Faerie Aislinn

Time Fairy

A Novel by Sterling J. Badon

00311231

ISBN: 9798866455683

Time Zones

PROLOGUE

Once more, we find ourselves In the rolling green hills where farmland and forest mingle, near a small remote town. This time, and most assuredly, I do mean time. We find out about Aislinn. Well, maybe not anything you ever thought you wanted to know, but you will be told anyway. And some things might make more sense because if you know anything about the magical world, it doesn't make sense, at least to a mortal person. So, if you dare to find out if you have an enchanted understanding. This story is for you.

Faerie Aislinn

Time Fairy

Chapter One

LEPRECHAUNS

HAVE you ever noticed there are no girl Leprechauns? None. Not a one. Anywhere. Well, Finn noticed. His Mother was a Leprechaun as far as he knew. And so was all of his friend's Moms. But there were no girl Leprechauns. Not even one. Their Mothers were once girls, but they didn't talk about girls or ever being one.

One day, Finn approached his Mother after a day of shaking corn stalks with his friends.

"Mom, where are the girl Leprechauns?" Finn asked.

She just looked at him and said, "Oh, My. That's a hard one to answer. There is no such thing as girl Leprechauns, but they are also all around."

That was all Finn's Mom said. She wouldn't offer anything more, and it was the same answer every time he asked. So, Finn went to ask his Dad.

The only answer Finn got from his Dad, if he even bothered to answer, was dismissive and reminiscent of what he received when his Dad didn't wish to deal with particular subjects, "Son, go ask your Mom. I am trying to make a tool to pick acorns, which has to be good. Those squirrels run and take them before I get to the good ones in the branches. Plus, your Mother has those answers anyway."

Finn left because he was unhappy with his parent's consistently obscure answers. He decided he needed to shake more corn stalks. Shaking any plant's stalk helped it grow strong and not fall over in the wind. It made the roots stronger. So he took his stalk shaking seriously. One of his friends liked to scare off caterpillars from eating the potato plants, and Finn wasn't fond of that. Corn stalks were his deal.

The Farmer was out in the fields today. This slight obstacle changed Finn's corn-shaking plans since the Farmer might see him. Farmers like snatching up little Leprechauns and trying to get wishes out of them. Finn always found that funny. Young Leprechauns couldn't even grant wishes. Boys could only make deals. Only an adult Leprechaun could grant wishes, which was dangerous for any Leprechaun to endure. He figured he would stay away from the Farmer. Humans were not something he liked being too close to, although he was still very curious about them.

Today, Finn decided to sneak into the Farmer's house while the Farmer was occupied. He wanted to see what was going on and how they lived. In the past, Finn learned that people had boy and girl children. When the Farmer's children had birthday parties, he would see many little boys and girls. The Farmer and his wife had one boy and one girl. One was named Bobby, and the other was Janice. Finn usually watched them play outside in their yard. It never occurred to him until recently that there were no girl Leprechauns. He wondered what it would be like to have a little sister. Bobby seemed to pick on his sister but always was there to help her with stuff. He liked the idea of having a sister.

The sun started to go down, so the children got ready for bed, and the Farmer would soon return after working in the fields. Finn could have just popped back home, but he figured he would walk in the cool night air that started to move in as the sun went down. There was no urgency to go straight to bed the older Finn got. His parents began to trust he would be safe and didn't worry so much.

Along the trail on his way home, Finn saw many fireflies. There was one that seemed to fly around him almost constantly. It was very bothersome, but he didn't want to swat at it. Because he would never hurt bugs. Knowing that they helped pollinate flowers and plants, which helped everything make fruits, vegetables, and seeds. Even if they didn't help them grow, they still were helpful in other ways. He figured if he ignored this firefly, it would eventually go away.

Upon arriving home, Finn noticed his Mother fixing him a bowl of acorn stew. Leprechauns don't eat much and need very little. Usually, only vegetables, seeds, and nuts help a Leprechaun connect to nature. Most importantly, they tried to only eat food grown on lands they lived on.

Placing the bowl on the table before him, his Mom said, "How did your day go? I hope you got lots of corn stalk shaking done."

Finn just hung his head and ate his stew. Finn's Mom looked over at his Dad, sitting in his chair by the fire, trying to read his paper. The paper was a shrunken newspaper from a nearby town. His Dad always liked reading the Almanac section and laughing at their predictions of crop production and the weather.

His Mom spoke up and said, "Dear, you need to tell Finn about girls."

Finn's Dad had a look of horror on his face. "Anything but that," Finn's Dad thought.

Finn looked at his Dad with a look of shock and said, "What's this?"

He smiled slightly because he knew his Dad was being forced to spill the beans.

Finn's Dad waved him to sit by the fire on the corn silk rug in front of his chair. Then he sat straight in his chair and said, "My beloved son. Boy and girl Leprechauns are different. They are not different like human boys and girls but in almost unexplainable ways." Finn looked on, puzzled, still not understanding what his Dad was trying to say.

"What do you mean by different?" Finn asked.

"Well, my son, there is no such thing as a girl or a lady Leprechaun!" His Dad stated as a matter of fact.

Finn just sat there looking at his Mom in the kitchen area cleaning up. "What do you mean? Mom is right there." Finn said, pointing at her.

Finn's Dad just laughed and said, "It will be clear one day. We are magical creatures and are not like people. Your Mom wasn't born like you or me. One day, she just appeared to me, and I couldn't get her to leave."

"OK, that's enough silliness for tonight. Finn is probably more confused now after what you just said." Finn's Mom stated, looking at his Dad.

"OK, Finn, time for bed." His Mother said as she shooed him away. Then, all of a sudden, Poof! Finn disappeared. Then Poof! He arrived in his room. His room was inside a hollowed-out branch at the top of the tree. He climbed into his bed filled with wool fluff he gathered after the Farmer sheered his sheep.

Finn tried to go to bed. He lay there, trying to figure out what his Dad told him about Leprechaun girls. Nothing! He knew nothing! Why so secretive? Why are there no girl Leprechauns? He pondered. He was tired from his long day and finally nodded off as he snuggled into the wool fluff.

The following day, he woke up at sunrise because Finn felt like causing mischief occasionally. It's what most Leprechauns long to do. So, he ran to where the Farmer's little boy and girl got on their school bus. Finn scared a ladybug towards them, and it landed on Janice's arm. Bobby went to squash it! Finn almost jumped out to stop Bobby when his hand was raised to squash the bug. He was relieved Janice had stopped him by simply turning away.

His joke didn't go over so well, and he thought the children would run. Because they usually did when he sent bees. No bees were around, so he tried that ladybug. Finn was worried for a bit since ladybugs are beneficial for the crops. They keep the crop-eating bugs away. They can be very cantankerous, and he was sure that should have scared Janice! At one point, Finn thought he saw Janice looking at him. So he disappeared into the vanishing, but she still seemed to be looking at him.

The bus arrived, so Janice let the ladybug off into the tall grass near the mailbox before getting on the bus with Bobby. Looking out the bus window, Janice seemed to wave at Finn. He was invisible. He had vanished. Did she see him?

"I'm telling you, Dad, she saw me! She was looking right at me and was also waving." Finn said back home as his Dad worked on another tool in his shop.

"Don't worry, Finn. Human children see us all the time, even if we are invisible. They usually forget right after. They can't even say anything to others, even if they notice us. It is almost as if they enter a dream state when they see us. It is like when we have a dream, but it vanishes quickly as soon as we wake. That is how they remember us. It's the adults that are a real concern. They can't see us if we are invisible, but if they see you when you are not. They come after you."

Finn's Dad seemed to be remembering a stressful event. He continued, "When a Leprechaun is being chased, we kinda forget we can go invisible. It is something that takes concentration. So adults who get aggressive towards us might catch us. We get afraid of being caught, so we forget we can vanish. It's when they grab us that it gets horrible. Usually, we can disappear or pop off somewhere else. We forget we can or can't concentrate on leaving when under duress.

Once caught, we are slaves to the wishes or a deal. Usually, we control deals, but once caught. They can ask for one if they know how. Most times, they go straight for the three wishes. That's usually all they know they can get. But if they know about our deals, it can be much worse because they can control us for many years, which is frustrating."

Finn let his Dad vent. He knew the Farmer almost caught his Dad a few summers back. The experience still made his Dad shutter. It was best his Dad let this out. So Finn just listened.

It had been days since Finn played with his friends. They came by his parent's treehouse and tried getting him to help them with their chores. Finn was good at assisting others to do a better job and at a much faster pace. Although he liked helping nature, today was different, and what had recently happened engulfed his thoughts. A person had seen him.

Did that little girl see him? Then there was the issue of him still not understanding why there were no girl Leprechauns. He had snuck into town once and saw many human girls. He also saw some on the bus Janice and her brother rode in. Then there were the birthday parties the little boy and girl had. He kept thinking about all the human girls of all ages he had seen. With these thoughts spinning in his head, he didn't feel like doing anything. This caused him to muddle most of the morning aimlessly.

A point came when he couldn't waste any more daylight. Finn finally went to help his friends with their chores. He didn't do a great job, but at least he showed up to help his friends. He couldn't get the fact there were no girl Leprechauns out of his mind. On his way home, Finn walked through a patch of daisies. Suddenly, a bright green flash appeared right out of nowhere and crashed into him! Finn tried to see what hit him through the sparkly pink dust falling all around as he tumbled in the soft soil.

"Oh, I'm sorry." A tiny little voice said from behind him. Standing up, Finn dusted the pink sparkles off his clothes. He then turned and saw a girl! She was about his size, which was only about six inches tall. It was a girl, but she had wings on her back like a dragonfly. "Hello. My name is Rosea," she said.

"Where did you come from, Rosea? What are you?" Finn asked.

"Well, Finn, I am a Fairy and your new friend." The feisty little Fairy stated as a matter of fact.

"Wait a minute, little Miss Rosea The Fairy. I didn't tell you my name. How did you know my name?" Finn insisted.

"Well, if you must know. I have always known you. Remember that firefly that kept bugging you the other day? Yep, That was me." Rosea said with sass, "I have known you for many years. I finally decided to let you see me. You are the only Leprechaun I have let see me. Until now, I was invisible unless seen as a firefly."

"What do you mean you have known me for years?" Finn asked.

"Silly. You are not a people. You are much older than those children you pester in the morning as they go to school. You are even many years older than those children's parents. You're a Leprechaun. I've been watching you for a very long time. And if you were human, you would be considered a young adult." Rosea stated as she skipped around Finn, tugging on his jacket and poking him with her finger here and there.

"OK, now stop that!" Finn stated as Rosea pulled on his orangish hair.

"Do you wash? Is this a piece of wool fluff?" Rosea said as she smirked and held up a small wool fiber she had picked off his dusty green jacket.

"You sure are a pesky little thing. Where do you live?" Finn asked.

"Well, I live everywhere," Rosea replied.

"No. You must have family and a home?" Finn requested.

"Silly, Fairies don't have a home. We live everywhere, and we don't have a family. We just wake up in a flower blooming one day and are born. That is it. We Fairies stick together, as you can see by all the Fairy firefly lights around you. They are making sure you're friendly." Rosea said, shaking her finger at Finn.

"Meeting you has been nice, but I must get home. My Mom will be waiting to serve me dinner. I must not be late." Finn stated.

"Nice talking to you, Mister Finn. Tell your Mom I said hello." Rosea said as she vanished, and nothing but a small firefly-looking light whizzed away.

"But, where can I find you?" Finn said as the small light disappeared into the distance.

Upon getting home, Finn told his parents about meeting the Fairy. Instantly, his Mother had a smile on her face. She knew Fairies were rare, and a Leprechaun never sees one unless there is a reason. That's what she had always told Finn. And this was the first time Finn had ever seen one.

Finn's Dad sat near the fire and said, "Well, this should be interesting."

"Interesting? OK, Dad, tell me what you mean?" Finn said.

"No, my son, you will have to figure this out on your own. I will tell you one thing. You can't get rid of that Fairy. No matter how hard you try! Those things are trouble. I do not want any part of that pesky thing." Finn's Dad stated.

Chapter Two

THE DARK ONE

SEVERAL days passed, and Finn would see Rosea occasionally, but she always vanished before he got close to her. He saw the firefly lights but never observed an actual firefly bug! It was just the light.

He figured it must be her friends watching him. One day, Finn was helping his best friend, Kieran. This day, Finn was learning to enhance the fertility of the soil. Kieran was from a family of Leprechauns that helped make the soil rich and dark. Usually, anything would grow well after Kieran or one of his family members enchanted the ground. Kieran was known as The Little Dark One.

"Hey Kieran, Why do they call you The Little Dark One?" Finn asked, looking at Kieran with one eyebrow slightly peeked up.

"Well," Kieran stated, all slow and mysterious, before finally saying, "It all has to do with my power to enhance the soil. It is something I am hoping to show you. The one catch is you will have to, at times, live like a human! This can be tricky and only something I have just started doing."

Finn looked at Kieran in disbelief, saying, "Are you joking? Don't we die faster if we live as humans?"

"That is true, but Leprechauns always find a way out of dying fast. Plus, we just need to stay on enchanted lands. That's what my Dad always says. We have friends who are already living large, as it's known. They are enormous! They do visit in their original size when they come to the woods, but they are often huge when in town." Kieran stated as he picked a four-leaf clover and nibbled on it. He handed it over to Finn and told him to eat a leaf.

"Nasty!" As he ate the cloverleaf, Finn stated, "I never saw what you and your family liked in eating clover. Now the honey your family gathers is fantastic. My Mom likes it when your family visits and gives us some. I had some in my milk last night, and that cow didn't like giving that up to my Dad!"

"So you see, Finn, the clover for us is just as important as the honey. The water we all drink from the creek is also important, but you had the cow's milk, which works since the cows drink from that stream. We can do many things that help the earth with a few items; honey, creek water, and a little clover is all that is needed. It allows us to help the soil quality, making it dark and healthy with nutrients and energy that help the Farmer's crops. I also do the same for wildflowers, plants, and forest areas that need help, making everything green during the summer around our homes." Kieran said this as he walked into the cornfield, knelt down, and held his arms forward. As Kieran opened his mouth, a sparkly silver stream of glittery light was emitted. It hit the soil, spreading evenly across the ground as it shot through the field.

It was dusk, and the Farmer thought he saw a light flash outside the window in the distance. People usually think they have seen light flash many times, but it happens much quicker than they can see. They typically dismiss what they might have seen and continue what they were doing. This is precisely what the Farmer did. He went back to paying his bills at his kitchen table. He figured it was a flash of a truck's lights through his window as they went by.

Finn stepped back as the silver light rushed across him as it shot across the field. Kieran stood up and looked at Finn as he said, "I feel so much better. Follow me, Finn. We need to go to another area and help the soil there."

Finn didn't say much. He just followed his friend, looking at how dark and soft the soil had become. He listened to Kieran tell stories of enchanting the dirt with his brothers. Many of his brothers no longer lived in the Leprechaun form. They were humans now. Well, They were in human form, enormous and big enough to have cats as pets instead of being snacks for them.

"Here we are. Now, Finn, it is your turn." Kieran said as he looked at Finn.

Finn looked at Kieran and nervously said, "What do I do? I don't feel so good. Should I be doing this? I think I am becoming sick!"

Kieran laughed kind of sinisterly and then lightheartedly chuckled as he pointed out into the distance and said,

"You see that out there, Finn? That's what you will help. It's not crops like I just did. Crops are very taxing on one. That takes so much energy and effort that you will do this simple thing for your first attempt."

In front of Finn was an opening in the trees. Beyond that opening in a clearing was a pond the Farmer had dug up and made many years ago. The levy around it had some grass growing on it, along with some flowers. It was getting darker outside, and Finn could see stars starting to form in the sky. The air got slightly crisper, and the two approached the pond. They were on the levy. Leprechauns don't like large bodies of water. They can't swim and fear being eaten by huge fish. It would need to be a giant fish, but that never stopped them from having an excessive fear of being eaten.

However, if a Leprechaun ever ate anything besides vegetables, nuts, seeds, fruits, or herbs, it would be the tiny minnows they would catch in the ponds nearby. Catching minnows was a rare event, and many Leprechauns would go together and treat it how humans treated hunting for a bear!

It was a big deal besides eating the fish on special occasions. They also used the minnows to lure cats away from areas they wished to enter.

Finn wasn't sure about this. He was nervous and just felt ill. Standing on the top of the levy, he kneeled. Finn felt drained, and standing was just too much.

Kieran stepped beside Finn and said, "It's OK, Finn. You will see. Just imagine this pond looking better. Imagine the grass on this levy greener than it has ever been. Even imagine the flowers, plants, and trees around this pond healthier than you have ever seen them. This area has not been enchanted for a very long time. We must do this even though we fear the water and the giant fish here. The ecosystem feeds the fish by keeping the plants healthy, bringing all kinds of bugs that the fish eat.

The Farmer fishes and catches large bass at times. It is his way to relax. Although we fear being caught by the Farmer. He is very respectable. We shake his corn crops and even help with his other farm items. We are in harmony with any human who cares for and treats the land well. That's what my parents always told me. There is no need to stress. You will do fine. You can do everything right here. You might do shoddy work, but you can't do anything that will harm you or this pond area. So relax, lift your arms forward, and consider making this place more excellent."

Finn lifted his arms and felt this uncontrollable urge to make this pond and the area healthy and beautiful. Even though it was at dusk and it was hard to see much. Finn saw everything light up as if it was daylight! He saw the pond, trees, grass, and flowers all bathed in sunlight. The light came from his mouth and was the same silver sparkly stuff he saw come from Kieran. It hit the pond's water and shot out in every direction. Then, in a flash, it was dusk again. He no longer saw the area lit up as if it were daytime. He realized he felt good. He felt better than he had in a very long time!

Standing up, Finn said, "Wow, If it wasn't for having to eat that clover. This would be awesome to do all the time.?"

Kieran laughed, saying, "Yes, it is pretty awesome, but you must endure the bitter clover to enrich the soil. Let's not stay here any longer than need be. I don't particularly enjoy walking near a pond at night. We could fall in."

Finn was in very much agreement. So the two said their goodbyes and decided to head home.

The following day, Finn woke up to singing. It was soft and gentle. It was pretty and made him feel all warm and fuzzy. He looked up towards his window, which was just a knothole in the tree branch. Finn saw Rosea sitting in that knothole, holding an acorn shell. She then dumped the water it contained onto Finn! Then Poof. She vanished!

Finn looked out the window, went downstairs to where his Mom was, and said as he looked around, "Where is she? Did you see her?"

Finn was sop and wet. He was frustrated, and he was soaked. Being wet was not something Finn enjoyed. He only bathed once a year. This was when water gathered in the crook of the tree during early spring. He only washed that one time during that year. Finn's Mom was laughing. She knew what happened. She knew her son was dealing with a Fairy! It would be nothing Finn had ever dealt with since Fairies can be a true force to be reckoned with. Finn grabbed dry clothes and got changed. He was just frustrated. Who was this Fairy? Why was she messing with him?

Finn decided to take a walk after listening to his Mom chuckle occasionally. She was laughing at him! What was so funny?

Finally, Finn decided to head towards the pond he visited late at dusk on the prior evening. He stomped his left foot twice and ended up in the forest clearing that led to the pond. The morning sun filtered through the trees. Bugs darted across the water's top. A fish tried to get a bug or two by popping at the water's surface. Then he heard that soft song again. It didn't have words, but he knew what it was. It was that bratty Fairy Rosea. He listened to her singing, but he didn't see her anywhere. Maybe it was the breeze? Perhaps it was just the shell shock of being dowsed with water earlier.

The song stopped. Then he heard a light giggle that faded away in the distance.

Suddenly, the grass around the pond seemed to get greener as he headed up the levy. He watched as the trees grew new buds. Then, the flowers near the pond started to open up and bloom. The few lily pads in the pond had flowers shoot out of the water and bloom at the surface. Where Finn stood, a ring of small white mushrooms grew out of the ground around him. In the distance, Finn saw a Fairy light swirl around after coming out of the woods, and it then glided across the water towards him. A fish tried to get the light and missed. Then, as this light headed towards Finn, the light turned into Rosea as she slid across the water's surface onto the levy. This sprayed water all over him. She stepped towards Finn and then picked a piece of lily pad off his face.

"How are you doing, Finn?" Rosea said as she pretended to dust herself off. She wasn't even wet. She just was showing off.

"Wet! I am Wet!" Finn stated as he looked at her, trying to figure out what was up with this Fairy.

Before Finn could vent more of his anger of being wet, Rosea blew a handful of fairy dust over him, and not only was his clothes dry. He was clean, his hair fixed, and his old tattered clothes were new. Finn could swear he smelled like dandelions! And he liked dandelions.

"How's that Finn?" Rosea said as she stepped closer, giving a quick, small peck on his cheek.

Finn wasn't mad anymore. He didn't know what to feel. He was no longer wet and was clean without scrubbing with soap and water! Plus, she kissed him! He had no idea how to act. Then, before Finn could ask her what she was up to. Rosea turned into a firefly light and wisped away.

Finn stood there, looking at the beautiful pond area and everything being exceptionally green. He was amazed at the fairy ring of mushrooms around his feet that had turned red and how he smelled clean! He couldn't remember the last time he smelled this good.

Later that night, Finn found himself around a fire with his parents, all the area's adults, and Kieran. It seemed like a huge deal, but no other boys were there. There hadn't been this many people visiting his home since they met about the Farmer bringing a cat home for his children. That's what the Farmer told his wife, but it was actually to catch mice. He knew something was getting into his food pantry. The cat was there to capture and kill those rodents.

That's when the Leprechauns started to catch minnows to distract that beast! They needed flour and a few other items. Mostly spices they couldn't find in the nearby areas. They were small people, so they didn't take much. But the Farmer knew something was getting into the food storage area! It was the fact that some containers had not been closed well or that flour and sugar would be found on the shelves. The flour had been tracked everywhere and into places where only a tiny animal could spread it.

Finn's Dad stood up, "Everyone is trying to guess why we are here tonight."

Then Kieran said, "No, we are not, as he looked at Finn."

Finn's Dad replied. "OK, maybe not everyone, but at least Finn is wondering why we are here!"

Finn's eyes widened as he looked around, and it seemed everyone was looking at him!

"What gives? Why does everyone know what's happening but me?" Finn said, feeling very uneasy.

"Well, my friend. You went and got yourself in trouble, didn't you? You couldn't leave well enough alone." Kieran said, disappointingly shaking his head.

"What? What could I have done? I have no idea what you are talking about." Finn said as he looked at his Mom, hoping she would rescue him from this.

The only thing that happened was Finn's Mom finally spoke up and was smiling, "My son is growing up. When he asked me why there were never any little girl Leprechauns, I knew he was ready for the truth. It is usually hidden for a reason from our young. Except for Kieran. He seems to be a loaner and always knew this and why he is here now."

Finn's Mom smiled even more as she said, "My son is finally a man," and hugged Finn and let Finn's Dad talk.

Finn's Dad sighed in relief and said, "I was worried. I remember when I was selected. I never understood why it all seemed so confusing. Till everyone gathered like this to celebrate my selection."

Then, out of the dark woods, several firefly lights wisped around and moved around everyone. One of those lights moved slowly around Finn, and then Rosea stood beside him. Rosea was in a beautiful white dress with flowers in her hair. Her wings lightly fluttered with small movements but quick little flutters. When Finn looked at everyone else around that fire, he realized his Mother now had wings. Every lady around that fire now had wings!

Finn turned towards Rosea and was instantly in a white suit. She reached out to hold his hands. Although unsure of the outcome, he realized he wouldn't fight it. Finn held her hands. That soft song he heard that morning rang out again.

Finn felt it calling to his soul, and he longed to listen to that song. And that song was coming from Rosea.

Kieran stepped towards Finn and Rosea and placed a ring on each of their hands. It was a simple ring made from gold that looked like a beat-up piece of wire. Kieran got back into the circle, and everyone held hands. The Fairy lights glowed brighter, and the Mother's wings even radiated soft green light.

Finn's Dad spoke up, "Finn, You probably are going along with this like every other Leprechaun has done for centuries. You know this is right, but you need to understand why. You are a magical creature. You are bound by our laws. You questioned why you never saw girl Leprechauns because you realized you were about to be paired by the powers that guide us all.

You didn't choose her, and she didn't choose you. At the same time, you both chose each other! This is how it works. That fairy ring of mushrooms signified you accepted Rosea's interest in you. The fact the area you enchanted bloomed when she was around you proves you were ready for this. You may now kiss your bride."

Finn knew what was happening but felt powerless to stop it. At the same time, he wanted this. Why? Why was this so natural? Finn looked at Rosea. She seemed to glow in a way he had never seen. Rosea was so attractive to him that he couldn't believe what he was seeing. She was otherworldly and stood there smiling as if she knew more than him. She had always known more than him! He understood that and was okay with it! He kissed her, and everything went dark.

Chapter Three

WHERE IS EVERYONE

NO campfire. No Fairy fireflies, No parents, No friends, No neighbors!!!! No Rosea! It was just Finn. He could barely see, but it was just because enough starlight and moonlight were coming through the trees. It was just him. He could feel the slight warmth of the fire that just went out. He didn't know what to do.

Then Finn heard that singing. That beautiful, soft singing. He saw a single firefly light come out of the woods again. It was Rosea. He knew this, but this was before she landed and became a Fairy.

"What is going on?" Finn asked, "I am kinda confused, yet it seems natural."

Rosea, still smiling, said, "Well, we have been selected to complete enchanted duties. I am your wife now. You actually chose me. You might not realize it, but you could not have seen me unless you wanted to marry me. And I have known of you for many years. Until you were ready, I was not visible to you. Oddly, I only knew stuff up to the marriage part. I do not know beyond this. I don't know what is happening. A Leprechaun just contacted me to visit him in another county. We are to move there and begin our lives. We are under enchanted law to move and can not visit here again until we finish our responsibilities."

"What does that mean? I just got married. I am happy somehow, but this is huge! It happened very fast. How can we trust this Leprechaun that just contacted you?" Finn asked, looking concerned.

Rosea stepped closer to Finn and handed him a card. On the front of a dark green card was a large golden L. and inside was a message that read;

"Hello,

I am Lyreman. I am the one in charge of this enchanted district. You two have been touched by magic to do enchanted work and will need my help. You can return home when your duties are completed. When a Rolls drives up, please get inside; it will take you to me in a nearby county. I will explain everything when you arrive. Enchanted Law has commanded this.

Lyreman"

Finn looked at Rosea, "How can we trust his letter?"

Rosea was unsure as she said, "When I first woke as a Fairy in a flower as it bloomed countless years ago. I found this card in my pocket, which was the only thing I had. I remember reading it and placing it back into my pocket. And only now, many years later, when I reached into the pocket of my wedding dress as you kissed me, I felt this card. I haven't remembered this card since I put it back into my pocket countless years ago. This card is the only thing that makes sense.

I have seen many people marry into enchanted relationships. And not one was ever sent away. They usually live near or around family. I disappeared because I tried to find everyone fast using my Fairy speed since everyone vanished immediately, and you were stunned for a few seconds and unresponsive! Your parents are not home, and your friend Kieran was not home either. No one is home. I even went to the forest where the Fairies in the dream state hang around. They are nowhere to be found. I can move at unmeasurable speeds in the dream state. In a blink of an eye, I looked everywhere. And nowhere I checked did I find anyone. Anywhere. We do not have a choice. I was born with that card! I always thought that was odd. It must mean something. We need to go with this person driving this Rolls."

As soon as Rosea finished her comment. A beautiful silver and black Phantom Rolls Royce pulled up. The driver stepped out and walked around to open the doors for them to get in the back. When they were in, the driver closed the doors, got in, and drove off.

It was a tranquil ride. After a few minutes, the driver said, "Hello, you two. I am The Butler. I am sure you are anxious about this situation, but rest assured. You will understand and agree this will help everyone."

Finn spoke up, "Why did everyone disappear? How could everyone just disappear?"

The Butler looked at Finn in the rearview mirror as he spoke, "Finn, I apologize for not having all the answers. I am taking you to the person who does. We will be there in a few hours. So try and get a little rest. Lyreman will answer your questions soon enough. You are safe and will be fine."

Finn and Rosea held each other for comfort, and neither would close their eyes. They didn't trust anyone, but they knew that note was their only clue to what happened.

The Rolls was their size when they were picked up and became human-sized as it drove off–leaving them as tiny individuals in the back seat.

Upon arriving, the Rolls was small again, and The Butler let the two out of the car. He walked them to the door of an ancient cottage. It needed lots of repair. The Butler knocked on the door first, then just pushed it open. He waved both Finn and Rosea inside. Then, stated, "Lyreman will be here in just a moment. He had a few errands before heading here. I am sure he won't be long."

The Butler closed the door as he headed out. The inside of the cottage was quite dusty and had ancient furniture tossed around in it. The two were not used to being inside houses or abandoned cottages. They were used to living in trees and in nature. The knocked-over chairs were human-sized, and they really couldn't sit in them. They both sat on the front edge of the short fireplace stoop. The air was still and quiet inside the cottage, with no sound of the wind, bugs, or rustling leaves from the trees outside. Finn was also used to hearing the sounds of nature in his room at night from the knot hole.

Finally, the door opened up. There stood a small man in a very well-made tweed suit. He wasn't a tall man, but he was a man. Stepping inside, he stated. "No need to fear," since Finn and Rosea had already hidden inside the cold, dusty fireplace.

"I am Lyreman." He closed the door and then shrank down to their size. They came out of the fireplace covered in soot. Lyreman chuckled at the sight of them as he said, "I am so sorry, my children. I should have known better. I sometimes forget many forest-enchanted people do not know me. Let me do this again in your size. I am Lyreman. I am here to offer both of you an opportunity to start a wonderful life and help out all enchanted people with your magic."

Finn stepped towards Lyreman. "Why such the bother? Why send our family away and drag us out here? Where did you send everyone away that we knew?" Finn said in an almost angry tone.

"Relax, my friend. I am on your side. I have answers, but first, let me take care of the both of you." Lyreman said as he waved his hand in a small circle. Both Finn and Rosea were human-sized and cleaned of all soot. Plus they were in very nice clothes. They were very old-fashioned cottage-type clothing but nice and new. Lyreman was also back to his small human size. Lyreman waved his hand again, and all the furniture was put into its place, dusted and clean. The dirt and leaves on the floor disappeared, and shiny blue tiles lay underneath. A few candles lit up, allowing them to see each other better.

"Have a seat here, Rosea," Lyreman stated as he pulled a seat from the table. He also pulled one out for Finn and waited for them to sit down.

Lyreman took out his pipe and packed it with tobacco. He sat in a chair, smiling as he looked at the two of them. He finally snapped his fingers, and the pipe lit up. After taking a few long puffs, Lyreman set the pipe on the table and said, "Your family will be fine. I have nothing to do with them disappearing, but I can help you bring them back. I will tell you both a short story, and hopefully, it will help you relax and trust me."

Lyreman made cups of tea appear on the table, along with cakes and a few meat pies. He picked up his pipe and said, "Where are my manners? I know better than this." He then pushed the long pipe into the palm of his other hand, which made the pipe seem to disappear. "There," Lyreman said, asking them if they wanted sugar or cream. Both just sipped their tea and hungrily ate and didn't respond. They just waited for him to tell them what was going on.

"OK," Lyreman said as he continued. "I guess you wish to hear my story. First, you two are not missing family and friends. They are still in the same place they were when you were bonded together with Faerie magic. The truth of the matter is both of you disappeared! Not because of anything bad. Both of you have gone back into the past. I see the residue all over the both of you."

Rosea stood up and walked to a window. Looking outside, observing the stars. "What do you mean? Finn and I both traveled back in time?" Rosea said with a puzzled look as she turned towards Finn.

"No, my dear. Both of you snapped back to where you belong! This is about you, Rosea." Lyreman said, waving his hand over his cup and filling it with more tea.

Finn got up and realized he was bound to Rosea and that things hadn't stopped since she started coming after him. He stepped to the door and opened it. "I need fresh air," Finn stated as he walked outside, closing the door behind him.

Rosea sat back down and held her empty cup towards Lyreman, and he had it fill itself up. She took a sip, holding the cup with both hands and said, "Why me? Why did I have to come back? I don't remember ever being here?"

Lyreman looked concerned, saying, "I only know that both of you came back here. A Pooka told me long ago that a Fairy and her mate would one day return to me. And I would meet the Fairy when she was two different ages. This Pooka also stated that it would happen within the same day of each other. It was a confusing comment, and Pookas can be misleading if they sense you are not deserving. And this Pooka showed itself to me as a red-eyed horse, which can be distressing. But it seemed to be very concerned for your well-being. Time residue radiates from you, and I sense you are from another place, which only means one thing. You're a Time Fairy. Time Fairies like you are very rare."

"What about Finn? I am worried. He was having fun and was free just a day ago. I had watched him for many years when I finally decided I wanted to be his wife. So I approached him. When he created a Fairy ring on that levy, I knew he also wanted to be with me. He didn't realize it yet, but the enchanted magic knew. I am now regretting approaching him. I caused him much harm, taking him from his family. I never knew mine because I am a Fairy, and we never know our parents. I ruined his life. What will I do?" Rosea said this as she stared into how empty her cup was again.

Lyreman snapped his fingers, and her cup filled back up as he stated. "First, my sweetheart. You need to walk outside with me, and we need to find Finn. I am sure he, of all people, can help us make more sense of this."

Finn was in the front yard, sitting on the cobblestone fence. It was dark, but one could tell he had his head sunk down and looked distraught. They both stepped towards him, and he looked up.

"Don't worry about me Finn stated. I will be fine. I just need to adjust to all of this a bit. My Dad always warned me about Fairies. Stated that if one ever started bugging me, I was in for it! Well. He was right! I don't think he knew how right he was going to be. I just don't understand. I know Rosea was brought here and feel I was taken also since I am bound to her. I just don't understand why we were taken here." Finn stated as he looked toward Lyreman in the dark.

"Let's go back inside. I have more to say." Lyreman stated, so they headed inside, and he coaxed a fire in the hearth with a snap of his fingers. The night air had gotten brisk. Lyreman told Finn about what the Pooka had stated. Then they explained to Lyreman where they were from and the note.

"A note?" Lyreman asked.

"The note, Lyreman! You put a note in my pocket! Don't you remember that?" Rosea said as if Lyreman should have known since he had them picked up.

Lyreman knew that both were tired, very upset, and confused. On this night, they should have learned what it meant to be an enchanted person and bound to their mate. They missed out on the magic of it all. They missed the celebration and the understanding of enchanted magic bringing them together.

Lyreman answered Rosea, "I am sorry, my dear, but this letter you got from me isn't something I have written yet. It stands to reason that I will write that. I just found out where

I would send The Butler to get the both of you. But you were already picked up. I am sure this has something to do with Time Fairy magic. I need to think about this more. I will leave both of you here and ensure you have plenty of supplies. My little friend Dawn will show up and help the both of you. The rooms are furnished and clean. I did that when I first arrived. I didn't want you two living in a dirty place. Plus, those sheets were ancient and dusty. Why don't the two of you get some sleep? I will be back tomorrow."

As the sun rose, they woke to the smell of flapjacks and maple syrup. Finn entered the kitchen and saw The Butler cooking. Rosea had just returned from getting flowers from the yard to put into a vase on the table. Finn didn't question it. He just sat down and ate what was placed on the table. And it was good. He had never been human-sized and eaten so much food! He was hungry! He was used to eating a piece of bread crust or drinking an acorn of milk, and he would feel full. He found that his human body made him very hungry! Rosea also seemed hungry as she ate a stack of pancakes after watching Finn enthusiastically eat.

The Butler laughed, "I guess neither of you have ever been human before. It will take some getting used to. I have brought you some supplies and this bell." The Butler pulled a small brass bell out of his jacket pocket. It had a long handle, and he placed it on the table.

"Now, you both need to make sure you really need my help before you ring this thing! I am a very busy man, and I will drop everything if you ring this and will be here as fast as possible.

Now, make sure to put this stuff away before Dawn arrives. She is very finicky. She is great but can be odd about untidy items. Oh! Lyreman stated he has figured out a few things and that you two should relax. You are where you are supposed to be, and Finn will eventually see his family again." The Butler said this and started to head out, "I will be back at noon to take the both of you to lunch. It's Friday, and the local restaurant serves incredible traditional fare."

Rosea cleaned up as Finn started to put away some of the supplies in the wooden crates The Butler had brought. There were even a few sets of nice dress clothes in one box. Finn turned to Rosea, saying, "I am sorry if I seem sullen. I am actually pleased that you chose me. I instantly liked you the very moment I saw you. I couldn't wait to see you again, even if you seemed to be toying with me. I am just concerned about my parents and all of our friends."

"Finn, you don't owe anyone an apology. You are only in this mess because of me. If I never got you to bind to me. You would still be in the future with your family. You didn't deserve this." Rosea said with a tear in her eye.

"Don't worry, my love. We will get through this. Plus. It isn't bad here. This is a nice cottage, even if it needs repairs. I also really like being human-sized." Finn said as he turned towards the door because of a very low knock.

When the door was opened by Finn, a tiny girl was standing there with a basket of bread, and she just walked in without saying anything.

"You must be Dawn. I heard you would be visiting us today.", Rosea said, trying to get a conversation going.

"Yes. I am Dawn. I will be helping you two adjust to living here. I can clean and fix anything you wish me to. I enjoy helping, so please ask. Lyreman stated our place was already very well kept, and he knew a newlywed couple that needed my help."

Dawn stated that she would be taking the guest room attached to the kitchen. She placed the basket of bread on the table and started to clean. She pushed Rosea aside, finished the dishes, and moved towards the stove to clean off the batter that The Butler spilled onto the cast-iron stovetops. Dawn used a little stool to reach the high items. She was just a tiny little girl. She cleaned quickly and smiled the whole time she was cleaning. It was fun for her. She did move quickly, as her wings showed for a split second here and there at random.

Chapter Four

Faerie Aislinn

QUICKLY, the afternoon approached as Finn and Rosea walked in the nearby woods gathering mushrooms. It was an errand that Dawn sent them on so she could use the wild mushrooms in a potato, carrot, and leek pie later that night. The forest was thick and lush with lots of moss and lichens, with wild bog orchids growing on the edges of a little stream that ran through it. When they returned to the cottage, they dressed in the nice clothes The Butler had brought them. The Butler arrived exactly right after they were dressed.

As they got into the Rolls, they noticed a small box in the middle of the seat. A note attached read, "For the two of you. A little human spending money." Inside the box were six gold coins and some odd paper money. Finn put this all in his pockets since Rosea was wearing a dress.

They seemed to drive for a while even though the Rolls moved quickly. The car finally slowed down and arrived at a restaurant named Faerie Aislinn. It was a lovely two-story wooden building in a row of shops. Outside the front window was a charming brass bench. Everyone going in was dressed very nicely. The ladies in high heels easily walked across the old cobblestone sidewalks. The Rolls stopped in front and let them out.

"Go inside, and Lyreman will be sitting in the back corner." The Butler stated before driving off.

As Finn and Rosea approached the restaurant entrance, a little boy rushed up, held out a pamphlet, and waved it toward them. Saying, "You will need one!" in an adorable fashion.

Also Standing near the restaurant doors was a lady. She was tall and slender with iris-blue eyes and long strawberry-blonde hair partially held up with a head scarf. Her skin was light and perfectly unblemished, and she wore a dress one would expect to see on a Fairy Goddess. The lady was waving everyone into the restaurant while handing out pamphlets as she said to the little boy, "Now, Anders. Is that the proper way to hand out our lunch menu? Try and stand still on the side of the walkway, hold a menu out, and ask if they would like one." She turned to Finn and Rosea and said, "Hello, I am Aislinn, and that is my son Anders. Welcome to our restaurant. I hope you enjoy yourselves."

Finn and Rosea nodded to the lady, then entered the restaurant and were led by a hostess to be seated.

"Sit down, Sit down." Lyreman waved them to sit with him.

"I am glad you decided to come. This is my favorite place to eat. The food is so good. One could swear it's enchanted!" Lyreman said in a very friendly manner.

As Finn and Rosea took a seat, the little boy Anders approached the table and placed a few dessert and drink menus near them. He then ran off.

Lyreman smiled and said, "That's a cute boy. I foresee great things for him."

Then Lyreman turned to Finn and Rosea and said, "Order what you want, and don't worry about money. I have this bill, but Finn, I advise you to pay attention and see how humans pay for food. Now let me tell you what I now know. I now know that Rosea's letter is already in her pocket in the future. It was a lot easier than I thought it would be. The advice from that Pooka really helped me out."

Finn stated, "Seeing a Pooka is rare and eerily spooky from what I have heard. They can be helpful, and they can be detrimental. How did it help you?"

Lyreman smiled as if very proud of himself, "I saw Rosea as a Fairy firelight! While leaving last night, I saw her flying around your cottage's window. I figured she was drawn to Finn. She eventually showed herself, and I was able to talk to her. The cottage is on enchanted lands, so it was easy for me to have her take on a visual form since I am excluded from laws that keep her hidden. This made it very easy to hear what she was saying."

"Me? You saw me?" Rosea said, raising one eyebrow.

"Yes. I saw you, Rosea." Lyreman continued his story, "Your fairy dream state is where you mostly lived. You then saw Finn and wanted to meet him. When I got you to admit that. I told you I could help you find Finn if you promised to put a letter in your pocket and keep it until we meet again. It was an easy deal since you wanted to be with Finn."

Finn laughed, "You mean she took the letter and came for me in the future?"

"Well, Finn. Not exactly what I am saying." Lyreman said as he went on, "I told her where you lived currently. I knew she was a Time Fairy and would travel to you, but that wasn't what she was supposed to do. She probably found you in this timeline when you were much younger. I ensured she didn't get hung up on the later version who had already married her. You being here now is because she watched you for years and finally decided to approach you. A Fairy must be sure before approaching a Leprechaun and allowing herself to be seen.

The two of you are meant to be together. When a Fairy is drawn to a Leprechaun, it is for life and is usually guided by enchantment. I had to help the two of you get here to me. Plus, I gave her a letter you told me about, and it shouldn't be possible since you needed the letter to be here to tell me. It makes no sense, and I can only thank the enchanted force for guiding this for now. Rosea said she woke up with this letter in her pocket as if it was her first day as a Fairy. This also doesn't add up, but she could have had her memories wiped out if she tried to travel in time. It's the only thing I can imagine would affect her so."

"Lyreman, you are very knowledgeable. So, tell me why there are no Leprechaun girls! Why do Leprechauns only have boys, and then one day, a Fairy decides to bond with them? I am not complaining, but I am honestly curious. I am in this and have no idea what's going on." Finn said, hoping for some straightforward truth.

"First of all, Finn, you don't understand Fairies," Lyreman said.

"Who really does?" Finn said, snickering.

Lyreman looked at Rosea and then Finn. "You honestly don't understand Fairies. You do not know what a Fairy is. Fairies are not just girls! You think there are no girl Leprechauns, but the truth is. Leprechauns are actually Fairies! They are men or boy Fairies! That is meant to be confusing. It was done that way to make sure humans didn't know that Leprechauns and Fairies were meant to be mates. So, Finn, you are a Fairy, and your wife will not become a Leprechaun like you probably perceived your Mom was. That is a prevalent misconception most boy Leprechauns believe."

"Well, that makes sense. I knew the boys were being so self-important." Rosea said.

Lyreman said somberly, "The fact that Fairies live in the fairy dreamland before choosing a mate is why things must be this way. Girl Fairies and even boy Leprechauns can exist in the fairy dreamland. Not to be overly complicated, but it's mostly girls who enter the dream state and wait till they find a spouse.

Both of you were born in the fairy realm. You both lived on enchanted lands, and Rosea mostly lived in the fairy dream world. This is what I have figured out so far. And now both of you are new at living as humans.

Currently, we need to have Rosea remember how she travels. Because with that, The Butler will know about driving out to get you. He drove off the other night after telling me I would understand once he returned. This is all I know. You visited him and told him to come to pick you and your spouse up. From what he told me. You were older than you are now. The two of you probably start to age."

Finn stated, "Age? I am over 100 years old. What do you mean age?"

"Well, Finn. You and Rosea are both about 18 years old in human years. That's young by human standards, and I must make up a story to have people accept you. I am assuming that is why the two of you allow yourself to age a little. From now on, I will say Rosea is my younger sister's daughter. You are newlyweds, and I am helping you get started in life. That's a good story and should keep the humans fooled."

Rosea was smiling and said, "So you are our Uncle? How odd. At some point, we will figure out why it was so crucial we came here."

Lyreman said, "So that you know. You will hear clatter as Dawn works for you. But she can get anything you need. And when I say she can get you anything. I mean anything. She can even get you books on repairing things besides building materials. Just never ask her how she acquires items. Even I am baffled at times. So it's best just not to ask. Finn, I advise that you start working on the roof. This will become your job. If you get this cottage up and looking good. I will show you my plans for you. Now for Rosea. You will travel here to the Faerie Aislinn tomorrow and start in the kitchen as a helper. Your household needs to make money. That is the simplest way to do that until we establish the both of you."

"I do not know how to cook or make human food. What will I do?" Rosea stated.

Lyreman laughed a little, "Neither of you needs to worry. The Butler will show up to help and guide Finn. Plus, that bell he gave you is very handy. Please do not ring unless needed. He is swamped most of the time. You are not his only duty. But please ring him if it is necessary. Rosea, you will be more than fine. The owners of the Faerie Aislinn are great friends of mine. Aislinn will guide you.

Aislinn's husband named the restaurant after her when they got married. Till then, it was a family restaurant that served primarily burgers and other fast food. Now, it is a Restaurant that serves standard four-course meals. It is delicious, simple food. They offer bread with your drink. Then they bring you your salad. When your meal is ready, it comes out. Lady Aislinn comes to your table personally to greet you, and later, the busboy removes old plates. Then, they offer the fourth course, which is the dessert. My favorite is gooseberry pie. I hear they import this particular strain of berry from a distant land. So Aislinn will be your guide, Rosea. I trust her; it will help you learn more about human culture. Both of you are less well-rounded than some enchanted folk. You were both raised in a rural area away from most people. Mainly, Finn needs help. Rosea first existed here in our town and might have more information from her broken memories. I am hoping that is the case." Lyreman finished saying as he stood up.

"Are you going already?" Finn asked.

"Yes, my friends. I have much to do. I advise you both to sleep with cotton in your ears. Dawn will clean all night! She is relentless, but she does excellent work. The best part is it energizes her and increases her magic to be this helpful. So ask her for anything you want, even if you see a crack in a wall or a chip on a cup. She can mend it. She can bring you anything you desire. Just don't ask her about humans. She is particular about that. One day, I want to have her socialize and be around humans. It would really help her out. I promise things will improve, and we will return you to your families. It might be just visiting, but at minimum, it will be that."

The night was noisy! Dawn almost seemed to be intentionally hitting pots and pans together at times. Finn believed she was trying to be annoying. At one point, they were finally able to get to sleep. Upon awakening, they were amazed at what they saw. The cottage kitchen looked new inside. The stones on the fireplace looked clean of all soot and almost as if the fireplace was just made. A new-looking floor was practically unbelievable. Its tiles were shiny, the grout looked new, and the broken tiles were repaired like new. Charming images from when carts and horse-drawn buggies were being used were on them. The walls looked like they had a fresh coat of white paint. Even the cast iron stove was so clean it looked brand new.

The old wooden table was still old and beat up. But it was spotless and seemed smoother and shinier. The wooden chairs had been repaired, and brightly painted flowers were put on the top of the backs. What stood out the most was Dawn, who was passed out holding a teddy bear-like item with no eyes, made out of scraps of cloth, and it seemed so worn that most people would have discarded it. Dawn was curled up near the side of the fireplace, snuggling that poor doll. Finn picked her up, brought her to her room, and placed her under the covers. She was a child but did things that were not normal, even for an average enchanted adult. Dawn never let go of that doll, even while fast asleep.

The two displaced Fairies went outside and took inventory of where they now lived. Both were very comfortable being so large. They liked the ability to move large distances with a few strides, but their magic seemed almost useless in human size. So they just walked around the cottage and looked at what needed repairs and what they wished to change. Mostly, it was about what needed repair as soon as possible. Some parts of the cottage were almost beyond repair.

"Can I help the two of you?" Walking towards them was The Butler. He was all smiles, and they found that odd. He seemed to have a somber look about him usually.

Rosea quickly said, "This place will need so much work I am not sure Finn will be able to do all of it."

The Butler stepped closer where the two were standing in a wheat field so they were far enough back to see the roof on the back of the house.

"I see what you mean. Not to worry. When Dawn wakes up, ask her to arrange a delivery of more roofing reed and straw. While you are at it, ask her for books and instructions on thatched roof repair. Trust me. Dawn will get what you need. She might look like a small child, about seven or so, but she is ancient and knows many things. It is odd when she seems like a child learning things for the first time at some moments. Then, other times, she knows more than all of us combined. So just go with it. She has her moments. At least she never turned into a Sprite. I couldn't imagine that. Those little critters are something fierce. Well, Finn, this house chore is yours and mine when you get to a situation you need help with. Now Rosea, you will come with me to the restaurant. I am told you will start today, so we can get you learning basic human skills." The Butler stated as he started to walk out of the field towards his car.

"Later, my love," Rosea stated as she headed toward The Butler's car.

Finn had the look of distress on his face. He had never really fixed anything. His current skills included shaking corn stalks and other plants to help them and, recently, how to enrich the land. But repairing a cottage that seemed to be falling apart was more than he could imagine. The task seemed daunting. He walked around the place, taking inventory of what was there. He only ever helped his Dad make things, and he never made anything on his own. This was a house!

The Butler dropped off Rosea and told her to find Lady Aislinn. The Butler always referred to her as Lady Aislinn, and no one ever corrected him. Rosea walked into the restaurant and was taken to Aislinn.

"There you are. I have been waiting to see you again. Follow me to the ladies' changing room." Aislinn said as she walked Rosea through the kitchen, past the walk-in coolers, and towards the very back of the building.

A door with a sign read, "Lady Employees Only." The both of them entered the room. This room had lounge chairs and makeup counters with large mirrors. It was very lush and pleasant. Considering it was just for lady employees, the room was extravagant. Aislinn walked to a door in the back of the room and entered. This room was very simplistic and had divided areas for each person's coats, shoes, and personal items.

"This one is yours, Rosea." Aislinn pointed to a unit with a few uniforms and shoes, "We supply all the work clothes, and if they don't fit, please let me know. When you are ready, please come back out to the kitchen area. The staff all wear white and black uniforms. Even though we are not a fancy restaurant, we dress up and make the environment pleasant for our guests. The men must wear bow ties, and the ladies have frilly collars. They can wear straight-up collars, but you must wear a broach in that small drawer instead. Once you find uniforms that fit you, please put a few in your area. These will be kept clean for you." Aislinn opened and closed a little drawer in the clothes area to show Rosea the broaches and personals.

Changing clothes was very new to Rosea. She usually wore the same item all the time. It was always clean, and she liked it. Fairies could be very clean, as most chose to be. She had changed her clothes a few times as a human and needed clarification about why it was necessary.

After a few minutes, Rosea stepped into the kitchen. Many people were rushing about cutting vegetables, peeling potatoes, and some cooking items on the stove or the grill.

"There you are. I trust everything fit well.", Aislinn stated as she escorted Rosea to a table near the back of the kitchen and said, "Have a seat right here. I want you to roll the silverware in this bin into these napkins."

Aislinn rolled a few sets of silverware for Rosea to observe. She then stacked them into a tray on the table.

Rosea asked, "How many do you want me to make?"

"This might seem odd, but you will make them till the silverware runs out in this container. Just make sure to get the basic utensils in the rolls. You will do this for the next few hours. You will see the wait staff come and take what you keep making. The dishwasher will keep dropping clean items into this silver bin for you to roll up. If you run out of things to roll, you can walk outside for fresh air or hang in the Lady's Lounge area with other employees. If you get hungry, you may ask a cook for food. I will keep the chores simple and hope you watch others as they work. You will learn a lot from just observing. If you run out of napkins to roll silverware, go past the dressing rooms to the laundry. Clean napkins will be there for you to use. I will be around if you need me, but I believe you can handle this." Aislinn stated as she headed to the restaurant's dining area to accommodate guests.

Rosea rolled silverware. It was easy, and she usually ran out of items to roll in a few minutes. So she walked around watching others cook. She was given some soup at one point, and she was amazed at how good it was. It had shrimp in it. She had no idea what a shrimp was. Now that she was human, she was always hungry. And what little she did eat as a Fairy was vegetables, berries, or some other item she picked from a garden or nature. But now she had eaten a soup with shrimp, which was different from anything she had ever had.

"It's Rosea, isn't it? Come over here and stir this for me, please. I am Anders Sr. I am Aislinn's husband. At least, that's what she calls me. Mostly, I am the Chef, and she has taken over my restaurant and made it into a place where every local comes to eat and have a good time. My beautiful wife really has the knack of making everything better." Anders stated this as he stood to the side, watching Rosea.

"Keep stirring those sauces constantly, and don't worry about the silverware. The busboy will make some between table cleanings. From what I see, you will be my sauce helper at times. You keep doing that and stir the bottom of the pots so nothing sticks and burns." Anders Sr. said this, then walked away after Little Anders, who had just passed by, looking like he was up to something.

Back at the cottage, Finn was not having any luck. Dawn was awake and had several shipments delivered, which included thatch, reed, twine, wire, ladders, tools, and books. A few local boys showed up to help. Finn learned how to remove and replace the old rotten thatch and reed from the boys. They had helped fix many roofs and were told by The Butler that Finn needed help. The lads were a little younger than Finn but seemed very handy and showed him how to fix the roof.

Dawn kept bringing out drinks and sandwiches for them as the day went on. A massive pile of old thatch and reed was off to the side of the house. Finn mostly handed the boy's new thatch and reed and took the old stuff away.

The enormous job went very fast, considering the size of the roof.

When the guys were down from the roof, Finn asked them, "What do I owe you?"

"Nothing. We don't work that way." One of the boys said, "We will need your help on our roofs next week. Plus, we are not done with yours yet. Lots of tying still needs to be done. The roof can blow away when we don't tie the layers down. We will be back in a few days after the sun dries it some; you will be able to help with the tying then."

The boys left, and as they headed away, Finn turned to Dawn and said, "I never got their names. I was so focused on fixing a roof that I forgot my manners."

Dawn just laughed and pointed to Finn's head. He had straw pieces sticking out of his hair. He had straw all over himself.

That evening, The Butler dropped Rosea back home with more supplies before heading out again.

As Rosea entered the cottage, she saw that the place was even cleaner than before she left in the morning. Turning to Finn, she asked, "Where is Dawn?"

"The poor girl is tired again. She only knows how to work very hard and then passes out. She cannot work at a slower pace and save her energy. So, how did your first job go?" Finn said, smiling because Rosea was home.

Rosea looked confused and pointed at Finn's head, "My day was fine, but do you need help getting that out? I so wish I had my powers. Then I could snap my fingers, and that straw would disappear." as Rosea said this, she snapped her fingers. The straw disappeared from Finn's hair.

"Did that just happen?" Rosea asked, astonished.

Finn brushed his hands through his hair and felt no straw there. Till then, that stuff was tangled in his hair. He had struggled to get it out as Dawn laughed at him. That little girl was about everything being clean but refused to help get that straw out of his hair. She laughed at him until she eventually got tired of cleaning and went to sleep.

Chapter Five

ANSWERS NEEDED

"WELL, we need to ring that bell. I am at a loss as to what we are doing here and why we had no powers, but you used magic in human form. I thought that was not possible." Saying this, Finn picked up the bell on the table and rang it.

They sat outside on the front door stoop, enjoying the fresh air and each other's company, waiting for The Butler or Lyreman to show up.

The Rolls showed up, and Lyreman was riding in the back.

"Get in, Get in both of you." Lyreman waved the two in, and they got in back with him.

The Rolls sped off at an incredible speed. Before either of them could even get a word out, Lyreman spoke.

"I know. The both of you find yourself in an odd situation; you just were married, Finn lost his family, and

Rosea lost her Fairy friends. That might seem like a lot, but it all is important. Neither of you have any skills that are useful in human life. Shaking corn stalks isn't a job any human does, and enchanting flowers to bloom isn't a skill set, either. I have to get both of you to learn basic human skills. You will pick them up quickly and not even know it's happening. Just bear with it." Lyreman stated as he sat back and looked out the window.

The Rolls slowed down, and Lyreman and The Butler looked right. There stood a silver-haired lady on the street corner selling flowers.

"Who is she?" Rosea asked, seeing that both of them seemed very interested in her.

"She is someone I can not help currently. I wish I could. She is a Fairy that is allowing herself to grow old. It is a long story and not a very happy one. At some point, I hope Rosea can help us with this. Since she is a Time Fairy." Lyreman stated as he looked at Rosea, and the Rolls sped up again.

"Where are we headed, Lyreman," Finn asked as they drove through the town and started into the countryside.

Lyreman looked at both of them, "For some reason, we are headed to where the two of you are from. Well, where Finn is from. As far as I know, Fairy Rosea is from our town and originally traveled to see Finn on her own without any help from me. But since you two traveled in time, I had to send Fairy Rosea to where Finn lives since her Fairy form was obsessed with our Finn right here. This concerns me since you said no one was there, and I sent her there. I only understand things like causality and can see into a person and tell where they have been or what they might do.

Time travel is something I could improve at, and I have minimal experience with it. So, we will see if anyone lives where Finn is from. Why did they disappear when you only went into the past? The enchanted people should have still been around. It never sat well with me that only the two of you were there and no one else. Not even Fairies in the dream state."

The car headed into the next county where Finn was born and raised. It was getting dark, and Rosea held Finn as she drifted asleep.

"We are here." The Butler stated, and everyone got out. He just sat in the car and waited.

Lyreman looked at everyone and asked them to think about being small. He told them that until they did. They would be huge, and everyone would hide. So, both of them focused on being small again. They both missed it, but they also liked being human-sized. It was convenient. Although it was not very magical, it was handy.

POOF! Everyone was small and the proper size.

It was dark, but it was a full moon. So it was easy to see. They were at Finn's tree home. There was the fire pit that was lit up during their marriage and went out when everyone disappeared. It was out now, but it was warm from just going out like the night everyone had disappeared. The coals were still hot. This means someone had a fire going earlier in the day. Finn headed into the tree where his parent's home was. Inside, sitting on a couch, was Finn's Mom.

"Finn! Is that you? Why are you home? Is your Dad with you?" Finn's mother stated as she stepped closer and said, "Why do you look older? You look like you have aged a little?"

Lyreman and Rosea had followed Finn inside.

"Mom, this is Lyreman and Rosea. We are here trying to figure out what happened to us. Rosea is my wife, a Time Fairy; we have been transported into the past. When that happened on our wedding night, everyone disappeared. We have yet to learn where anyone was. Do you know what happened? This was just a few days ago."

Finn's Mom rushed up to Rosea and hugged her, saying, "I am so glad to meet you. What a delightful surprise. Even if it's out of normal time." Then she hugged Finn and said, "I am delighted to see you even if you are not my current son."

Lyreman stated, "I hate to cut this short, but we won't stay long if Finn's current self is returning! That can not happen. Those two must stay away from each other. Finn doesn't remember seeing himself already, so it must not happen, and we should keep it that way."

Finn's Mom stated, "I am sorry, I am Oona. It is very nice to meet you, Lyreman. Your name is famous to many. I can ease your stress a little. My husband and Finn will not be home for a few days. Most of us from this enchanted area are visiting a little boy in your town. They have been gone a few days and will all stay away a few more. I only stayed a day and came back. I had things to do, and it's a very emotional situation to deal with over there."

Rosea spoke up and sounded relieved, "That's good to hear. We thought everyone had vanished when we went back in time. I am sorry to hear you are dealing with a sad event."

Oona had everyone take a seat and continued to give details of what they were doing, "It's actually a happy event today. I am sure our future Finn remembers visiting the little boy Gustav. He was one of several who went to check up on the boy after what happened a year ago."

"Yeah, I do remember that. That was long ago for me and not just the other day. That was at that pub called O'Conner's, if my memory is correct. That poor boy. What a horrible thing. I still can't get over what happened back then." Finn said as he seemed to get very shaken at the memory.

"What happened?" Lyreman inquired as Rosea looked at Finn, concerned because he usually always smiles with a glimmer in his eyes. At this moment, Finn's eyes looked remote and lifeless.

Finn spoke up, "I'll tell you what happened. I am so glad that man is no longer around."

Oona interrupted, "What do you mean he is no longer around? He is still in the farmhouse. We have to be very careful of him and his son!"

Finn continued, "Well, Mom, you will not need to worry about that man much longer. I am unsure what happened, but one day, he left in an ambulance; I believe it was called. He never came back. His boy ended up running the farm from then on.

"Well, that is no better! He is just as bad as his Dad and just as dangerous!" Oona stated.

"I need to fill you in on things to make sense of this. I am unsure if it has anything to do with us traveling back in time, but it might." Finn went on, "Well, it turned out that the Farmer's son had been visiting a little girl in the cottage down the road. She was very nice; the boy had hidden that from his Dad. The boy was still very young but not lazy at all. Their farm was dying, and we know why, but I will get to that. The boy would help at a few nearby farms and earn money to help his Dad pay basic bills."

As Finn said this, Lyreman asked, "Why was the farm dying? What could kill crops on land that enchanted people were living?"

Finn sat back on the couch he was sitting in and said, "The farm at one point was doing exceptionally well, and the crops were healthy and highly productive. The Farmer's wife died, and the Farmer got very sad. Then he became angry at everything. This is part of why his son even hid that he was visiting his little friend. At one point, a family with a little boy visited us from overseas here in our forest. They wanted to live in the land of the enchanted's origins. They were all blonde with blue eyes and talked about the alpine flowers that grew where they were from.

They were willing to live in our community and learn our customs. Sadly, we didn't realize that Leprechauns and Fairies are not hunted where they are from. One day, the family was walking near a field the Farmer was in. He had hopped onto his running tractor and tried to drive them over. Many of us were used to that, and we would just vanish. We knew he would chase us and were prepared to disappear or pop to another place.

We believe they must have been stricken with so much fear they forgot to vanish or pop away. They just ran! Being small, they were run over. They all died instantly, and they just faded away. Except for the little boy, Gustav was being watched by one of us and was in a field in a basket while they picked berries. The Farmer was just angry he didn't get his wishes. He didn't care he had killed people. We could hear him yelling about it when his son arrived home. The Farmer's son was distraught that his Dad killed some of us. Although the son always tried to catch us and wanted to get three wishes, he would never kill anyone. We didn't think the Farmer would either till the day he had become violent."

Lyreman said, "Desperation drives some humans towards insanity. And this situation is very tragic beyond words. I knew of the little child Gustav being left at the doorstep of the O'Conner's pub and those untimely deaths. I did not think that happened at this farm, which eludes me. I see why the crops started to fail. Not many enchanted people have ever died that way. So where was the little boy, and why was he not small? His parents were both enchanted, and he was a full-sized human baby. I usually know everything where I live and the surrounding areas. I am at a loss here."

Oona spoke up, "That baby was only part enchanted. His father was human but started to become a Leprechaun because he married a Fairy. The baby always was the size the parents were. When they changed sizes, the baby automatically was their size also. When they died, he became an enormous child. We are fortunate he wasn't inside a tree or hill home we live in. That could have been even worse. He would never go back down to a small size. He was a human baby; no magic we knew would help him. We didn't know any family we could give him to, and we couldn't take care of him. We didn't want to give him to that Farmer who murdered his parents." Oona paused and breathed in slowly. She was upset at this, and it didn't seem she could finish the story.

Finn said, "I've got this, Mom. We had a huge baby and had to make a decision fast. Some of our people visited Aislinn since she was once a Fairy from our forest when she was in the fairy dream realm. She drove here to pick up the baby since we could not transport it there. Aislinn was friends with the pub owners and knew they had tried to have children for years and were never blessed with one. She knew they only had a few enchanted qualities. Still, she figured they would be great parents even if the little boy Gustav went into the fairy dreamland when he was five. It wouldn't matter since they would forget, and at least they had a child for a short time. Aislinn didn't leave the baby on the doorstep. The pub owners told everyone that, so Aislinn wasn't connected to it."

"Aislinn is a great lady. She is an asset to the enchanted realm. I just wish she and her husband wouldn't drive so fast. They act as if that car can stop on a dime. Always makes me nervous to see them drive." Lyreman said this like he said most things. Very straightforward and to the point.

"So how did the Farmer's little boy get the farm better?" Rosea asked, looking at everyone else. No one knew except for Finn.

Finn spoke up and didn't seem confident but mostly was apprehensive at what he asked, "The Farmer and his son still live in the farmhouse?" Finn looked at his Mom as he asked this.

"Yes, they do. Why is this important?" Oona stated, concerned since she knew her son and realized he planned on doing something dangerous, and she was scared.

"Since we don't need to leave before the current Finn who lives in this time is back home. It is important that I stay here and fix the land. And I believe I know how. That little boy would never harm me. But I am very sure he will try and get those three wishes!!! So I must help him." Finn said as he looked at his wife.

"Definitely not! I will not lose my husband when I just captured him! It took years of planning and whispering into his ear! I am against this!" Rosea stated with a very stern look on her face. That look was hard for her since she was a wonderful and kind person and did not have one mean bone in her body.

"OK, Rosea. Calm down. I know your concern, and I am also against what Finn wishes to do. But I honestly think Finn knows best. He knows those crops improve and doesn't want to share that information. I feel he also needs to know about your past. I think you need to tell him this." Oona stated.

Lyreman just watched on with interest. He wanted to fire up his pipe and get a few puffs but realized that would not be acceptable. He sat there taking in the information, realizing what Finn had planned was dangerous but might work.

Finn looked at Rosea and asked, "What should you tell me, My Love?"

Rosea looked at him and said, "Well, my name isn't Rosea. It's Niamh, and I knew your mother when she was in the fairy dream state before she married your Dad. She knew me long before you were even born. I have been in the fairy dream world for a very long time. Like the legend, I am drawn to Oisín, the son of Finn."

"I am named Finn, not Oisín. That is just what my Mom calls me sometimes." Finn stated.

"Not really, my son." Finn's Mom interjected and continued, "You are named after your father, who is also named Finn, but your second name is Oisín because we had a conflict calling you Finn when your Dad was around, so I called you Oisín. One day, I just started calling your Dad, My Love, or Old Man, and calling you only Finn. Your Dad was named after his father, who was also called Finn. So you are definitely Oisín, just like in the legend."

Lyreman chuckled and said, "No way! You two are Oisín and Niamh from the fables? I knew you two were special, but I did not see the energy of you till I learned this. I now understand why it is important I help you with things. Rosea took Finn away to another land or time, like in the fable. That makes sense. I believe I understand things better."

"I am a fable? Am I someone else? What does that mean?" Finn asked, looking at everyone.

"Nothing, my boy. You are still Finn. You were once a son of a great warrior and was stolen away." Lyreman stated this as he took out his pipe and fired it up. He needed to think, and that pipe was how he did that! He would just wait to be yelled at by everyone. So Lyreman continued his comment,

"You are just on another life. I have been through many. I am getting older, and I will start anew at any time. It is what enchanted people do. Even those poor enchanted people whom the Farmer killed will have another life. They will never know about the past, just like you don't remember. Your wife, on the other hand, is a Fairy born in the enchanted dream world and has access to old memories like I do. Many Fairies retain memories of their time in the dream world. It is part of how our world operates. I always wondered what happened to Niamh. No need to worry, Finn. I would be concerned about what you are planning to do. It is perilous, but I agree that it is needed."

Finn stood up and said, "Fine, I will do this. I know how things get better, and I am sure that this land in this time is cursed and needs a Leprechaun's help. Since I am married, I can do this and will have the powers of a grown Leprechaun. Rosea, I wish that you and Lyreman would both go back home and come back tomorrow night. But I have a feeling that neither of you will. So you will both need to keep a distance. If I remember the story, my parents told me why the land improved. They were vague, and my Dad only had partial information. I always thought he was avoiding the conversation, but I now realize he wasn't here for this. And my Mom always knew the truth, and everyone would ask her about what happened.

Although she told a good story, it always seemed she wasn't offering some information, and now I understand why. She couldn't. I am glad I loved that story and begged her to tell it to me repeatedly. She always told me how brave I was, like the boy in the story who healed the land when I was scared of things my friends were not scared of. The extra things she told me back then make sense because she knew I would need that information one day. I will need everyone to stay away from me tomorrow. It won't be easy, and I will need rest if I do this."

"Not till all of you have a bit to eat and something to drink," Oona stated as she brought out tea and items. She had scone crumbles, jam, rose hips, butter, honey, walnuts, sunflower seed kernels, and pansy flower pedals to roll stuff up with. Everyone ate, but Finn ate three times, which was tough to do as a Leprechaun. Because he thought he needed to eat. If he was to do what he tasked himself with, he needed to have the energy.

Once everyone finished watching Finn eat more than they had ever eaten in their enchanted forms, they headed to bed. Finn and Rosea went to Finn's room, and Rosea tossed all the bedding out the window and snapped her fingers. The bed had fresh wool and leaves to cover themselves with. Lyreman got into the Rolls and slept in the back seat. He had The Butler hide the Rolls, which had been shrunk to enchanted size. The Butler had seldom been small for long in the past, so he walked around most of the night, enjoying the size Lyreman made him.

"So I am taken away by a beautiful goddess?" Finn said as he started to drift asleep by Rosea.

Rosea kissed Finn's forehead and said, "Yes, My Love. I have tracked you through the ages. I keep finding you, and you occasionally leave to see your family. Nothing has changed in many eons. I am fine with that. I don't completely remember my past lives, but I always remember you."

As Finn drifted off to sleep, he was heard saying sleepily, "Sounds good, Dear."

Chapter Six

HERO TIME

EVERYONE was up early the following day. They didn't sleep well knowing what Finn had planned. And were unsure if it would be safe, but they knew it had to be done. The crops were dying, and that would force those living on the land to leave if they couldn't fix it. The enchanted would all need to abandon their homes and move to where the ground wasn't cursed.

Going out early to get the milk. Finn was amazed the cow could produce milk since the land was so sick. This allowed them to eat a breakfast of honey, milk, and oats, mainly consisting of just a few oat flakes placed in a thimble and soaked in a bit of milk with a very tiny drop of honey. Although not much, Finn had a second helping and hoped it boosted his abilities. He was in Leprechaun form, so it had to work.

When it was about noon, Finn told everyone to keep their distance. For this to work, he needed his mind to be nimble and couldn't afford to worry about them.

Finn watched the Farmer's son do his chores. He watched the little boy visit his friend down the road and how the boy picked wildflowers along the fence as he got closer to the little girl's house. She put them in a vase on their porch after smelling them. Then, that little boy went into those people's fields, fed their animals, and ensured their crops were watered. He was young, so he couldn't do more than that. Their crops looked okay but also seemed damaged from the curse of the actions of the boy's Father.

Finn also noticed how only the little girl and her Mom lived in the house. They had no one to help them do lots of their chores. At one point, the mother was out in the field on a tractor tilling soil for a flower crop she grew to help the homeless by giving them something to sell. The lady was of simple means and lived meagerly. Finn watched this little boy until late in the day when the boy headed home. That's when Finn knew it was time. If he was going to fix things. It would be now.

Finn jumped out of the tall grass on the side of the dirt road. He landed right in front of the little boy. And was just far enough away that he could run if need be. Dodging through the tall grass and beyond the fence would slow the boy down. Allowing Finn time to vanish or pop to another place.

"I can help you!" Finn said as he landed on the road.

The little boy was shocked at what he saw. Then he started to go after Finn. It was apparent that the little boy wanted those three wishes.

"STOP! I WILL GIVE YOU THE THREE WISHES BUT LISTEN FIRST!" Finn said, holding the palm of his hand out as if stopping traffic. The boy stopped. He just looked at Finn, trying to decide if he should grab him or listen.

Finn stepped closer and said, "I will grant you your wishes and also give you a deal if you listen to me. So let's get off the road where no one can see us."

The little boy didn't say anything but followed Finn. He had the boy sit under a tree in the nearby field so the Farmer couldn't see them. Then Finn told this boy how he would give him three wishes and a deal if he listened to him very closely. Being in Leprechaun form made Finn small and fragile, and being close to the boy put him in great harm's way.

The little boy asked, "What do you need from me?"

"Well, first, I can not give you my name. I wish I could, but since I can't, I will not use yours." Finn sat before the boy and continued, "I can make your farm healthy again. I think that is a terrific wish. I see how the crops are dying. I also see that your friend's farm is struggling to do well. I believe that would be a terrific wish also. I can not tell you what to wish on your third wish. I strongly suggest the first two wishes." Finn said this, and the boy leaned towards Finn. Instead of feeling fear, Finn felt the boy was feeling gratitude and almost relief.

"What do you need from me?" The little boy repeated.

Which was very insightful, Finn thought, because he did want something.

"You are right. I do want something from you. It will be your promise never to try and kill any of my kind again." Finn said.

The Little boy sighed and said in a low tone, "I am sorry. That was not me but my Father. I would never harm any of you. I would have tried to stop him, but he is always so angry. The crops are dying, and he has been sad since my Mom died. I am not sure if he realizes what he really did. I can promise you that I will never try and hurt you."

"That sounds like a fair deal, and in exchange, I promise to help you in any way possible if you keep your deal. That includes allowing you to have three wishes. I do have to warn you that even though I allow you to catch me for these wishes, It will terrify me. It is not anything a Leprechaun wants to happen, even though I am letting you do this. Now, I will tell you how to do this and will help you if you promise never to kill any of us living on your land. Plus, you can not tell anyone how you got these wishes." Finn said, seeing the boy was listening intently.

"I promise. I really need these wishes!" The little boy said.

Finn started telling this boy what to do, "Now, when you ask for your wish, think about it and only ask for that one item. Be careful not to ask for something I can twist the meaning of. It is instinct for a Leprechaun to give the least amount of what you ask. I want you to get everything you want because if the land is healthy, we don't have to leave, and you also live well."

Finn stuck his left foot forward as he stated, "Now when you grab my shoe, say, "I've caught you" and then ask your wishes very carefully and one at a time. You shouldn't ask for more than one thing in a wish because this will waste the wishes. And don't fear since I will disappear once the wishes are done. That is normal."

The little boy grabbed Finn's tiny shoe and said, "I have caught you!" Then he started to ask for his wishes. They were wordy, and any other Leprechaun would have taken the chance to lessen the wishes, but Finn wanted to help this boy. Plus, his deal helped him not trick the boy.

The boy said, "For my first wish, I wish our farm, crops, and home were healthy again. I am sorry for people dying.

My second wish is that my friend and her Mom's farm does so well, and they have enough money. My third wish is for my Dad to get better and not want to kill the Leprechauns that help our farm and my friend's farm, and not be so sad about Mom dying. I am done. Was that good enough?"

"Poof!" Finn disappeared in a cloud of sparkles as he said, "Your wishes have been granted."

Then Finn reappeared in front of the little boy again. He stuck his left foot out again and said, "You asked for a lot, so grab my shoe again. You don't need to ask for anything. I know what you want. Just say you caught me again."

As soon as Finn did this, the boy grabbed the shoe and said he caught Finn. Finn just disappeared again with no wishes asked for.

Finn showed back up and asked the boy to grab the shoe again.

"Why so many times?" the little boy asked when Finn reappeared.

"Well, my young fellow. You asked for a lot more than three items. You blew your initial first three on your first wish. So I am giving you the rest. Each wish was three wishes, basically. Plus, don't forget we had a deal, so that's why I can do this. Normally, you would just get the first wish since it asked for three things, and I would vanish from you forever. I am terrified, but my deal helps me keep my promise. Say it one more time. This is the final time." Finn said, and the boy repeated that he caught Finn one last time while holding onto Finn's shoe.

"Poof." Finn disappeared for good and was back home in his parent's tree.

Lyreman, The Butler, his Mom, and Rosea came to see how he was doing.

"I am fine, everyone. I was terrified, and it will work out, I believe. I am not sure that the little boy realized what he asked for. It will help him, but it will be a shock to him. I just wish I remembered to have him not get a cat in the future!" Finn said as he saw his Mom's eyes look shocked since all enchanted are afraid of cats in their small size.

Cats were known to torture an enchanted person if they didn't get away. The cat would play with them and then eventually kill them. Cats were not considered friends of The Enchanted.

Chapter Seven

GRIM DELIVERANCE

THE next day, an ambulance was heard at the Farmer's house. They carried the Farmer out on a stretcher. He was awake but was saying things that made no sense. Claiming that a red-eyed beast attacked him and Leprechauns took over his land. It started to rain as soon as the Ambulance left with the Farmer. Although the little boy seemed sad, that faded when Lyreman was given custody of the little boy. He claimed he was the boy's Uncle. Also, his friend and her Mom visited often. No one questioned Lyreman being the boy's Uncle even though Lyreman looked nothing like the boy or the Farmer.

A few years went by. The farm recovered, and the crops were so abundant that the money coming in also helped out the boy's friend and his friend's Mom. It didn't hurt that Lyreman had locals come and work on the farm. They got a portion of the crops and were happy since their crops had smaller yields and, for some odd reason, were not doing as well.

But presently, where they were, Finn and Rosea could never visit the area. They might see their younger selves, which could mess things up. Finn's mother, Oona, said she would be fine since her younger Finn would be home soon, and she wouldn't tell him anything about what happened. Everyone decided that would be best. What he did would scare a Leprechaun to death, much less Finn, living years knowing he would do that. Getting caught is the worst fear a Leprechaun has. Finn's Mom made him promise that he would return to her in the future. She would not see him again unless he did. Finn knew she would always see him. He would have to stay away until fifteen years passed and he could see them again. The younger version of himself was still there. She would never be without him.

The night after the wishes were given to The Farmer's son, as they headed back to their cottage, Rosea asked Finn, "So tell me again. Why did the Farmer have to leave in the Ambulance?"

Finn smiled even though he felt terrible for The Farmer. He was glad it made everyone safe, but it did make him sad. He replied, "The Farmer killed enchanted people with his tractor. The energy that was released was very negative. Besides the land absorbing it, that tractor transferred some negative energy to the Farmer. Which spread wherever he walked. Killing magic doesn't allow it to go into the environment around it.

Since The Farmer's son wanted the farm healthier. There was only one way to do that. His Dad had to leave the land because he killed someone and would never be free of the negative energy. Killing with ill intent is one of the worst things to ever do, and that will always be with him. Plus, The Farmer also needed help dealing with some form of depression. The Farmer will improve but must always live at a professional care facility. Although somewhat better because of his son's wish. But not even a wish can undo the evil of murder. He will live with that for the rest of his life. I felt that as I fulfilled the wishes."

"Did that boy deserve so many wishes? You gave him nine wishes and a deal! I know it helped to heal the land, but that was an exorbitant amount. Many Leprechauns have never given one set of three wishes. You gave him three sets almost as soon as we were married, which is as soon as a Leprechaun can give wishes. What were you thinking?" Rosea stated, knowing Finn had an excuse. And she wanted to hear it.

Finn smiled again. He knew Rosea was having fear flashbacks, and he wanted to ease her mind but didn't want to lessen the importance of what he did, so he said, "I didn't have to give him all those wishes, but it occurred to me that I knew this boy better than I realized. For many years, I thought this boy, as an adult, was trying to catch me. Those children I played tricks on were from when he grew up and married that little girl, his childhood friend. I always thought he was trying to grab me for wishes. I always just ran. The fear of being caught had me ignore anything I thought he said as he ran after me. Dealing with that boy, I realized he recognized me from his youth. He remembered me helping him. He probably just wanted to talk to me. It's tough to say, but I know in my heart he would never harm me. But he did buy that cat! And I wonder why he did that."

Finn and Rosea realized they were stuck in the past about fifteen years or so. Both of them wished they could have been able to at least visit the correct time for a few days. Rosea was a Time Fairy but had no idea how to travel. She transported both of them to the wrong time and was still determining if she had traveled when she was in the fairy dream state before she met Finn. She knew nothing about how her time travel powers even worked. Finn and her could not even control their size. Lyreman was the only reason they became human size and the reason Finn was able to become small so he could use his Leprechaun powers. Without Lyreman, they were both humans, and magic wasn't easy to do.

Back at their cottage, they decided to learn how humans lived. So Finn and Rosea shopped in the local stores over the next few weeks, visited church, and ate at local restaurants. The pub was a favorite. Of all places, it was not the healthiest of choices, but they liked the food. They had huge appetites being human, and until the last few months, they only had tried shrimp or water creatures, as Finn called them. Now, they ate burgers, stews, and things like chicken pies. They still ate lots of vegetables, but being so hungry, they sometimes resorted to meat. Human bodies were very demanding.

Finn would visit the farm area when everyone was asleep and enchant the land. Rosea would go along to drive him. Finn had made a deal with that little boy. That meant that he would help keep the land fertile and prosperous. Finn also did this to the ground around their cottage, but enriching this farmer's land brought him peace. Finn could only get smaller to enchant the land and make the crops grow. He usually returned to human size while Rosea drove them back to their cottage.

It had been a few months, and on one trip back from Finn enchanting the land, Rosea said, "I am not unhappy. We have a good life, and everything is going well. I know you wish to see your family, and you can't see the people here now. Your mother has talked to Lyreman, and they agree no one can know you went back in time and fixed things even though you are an unknown hero to everyone there. Most importantly, you saved the land you grew up on."

During this ride home, Finn had not grown back to his human size. He felt better after helping the crops but was very tired. So he just listened to Rosea as they drove in the night air. The old car Lyreman loaned them was handy, and Rosea was a far better driver. Finn preferred to drive slower than her, and at the moment, he couldn't drive anyway. Plus, she didn't mind the little red beat-up car that every kid in the area had learned to drive with. She thought it was cute and perfect as long as it didn't rain. This was because it was open to the air since the convertible top didn't work. One would need extra clothing when it got cold because the cute little car also lacked a heater.

It was a car from a company Lyreman invested in that could have done better. And all he had to show for those investments was that old, worn-out car. For a Leprechaun to fail at investments was almost unheard of, and Lyreman didn't discuss that. It was as odd as the times he was fuzzy on specific facts. The last several decades, or even more, were very vague for him. The only thing good about this car was that Lyreman kept it running, and the seat kept getting replaced. He insisted it was comfortable even though it was a very rough-looking roadster. And for some reason, magic would not restore it. It was enchanted never to break down, but the dents, dings, and rust never disappeared, unlike on the Rolls that The Butler drove. Another item that illuded Lyreman.

One good thing everyone had noticed was the Farmer's son was doing well. Lyreman ensured the boy was attending school and the farm was functioning correctly. He even found the sister of the boy's Mom. She stopped by often and helped the boy pay bills and arrange for other farmers to work the fields. Lyreman made sure she had any help she needed. Plus, she could make money and was working on moving into the farmhouse until the boy could live alone.

Driving down the road at night was very relaxing for Finn and Rosea. The simple life in the cottage, thatching roofs, and working at the restaurant was more hectic than either of them was used to. They were adapting and even started to understand human money. They were just constantly tired. In their enchanted form, being tired was always just a quick nap away, and then they did whatever they wanted to. Not now. There was a schedule. That must be followed, and if one didn't, everyone was upset, and things didn't work. So, both of them enjoyed the cool night air with the soft scent of flowers growing in some areas they passed. They also started to notice Fairy lights dancing across the fields that lightly touched the tops of the wheat and other crops.

"DID YOU SEE THAT?" Both of them exclaimed at the same time.

They looked at each other and just smiled. Rosea saw the lights as a human, and Finn saw them in his enchanted form. Then, Finn slowly became his human form again. Looking at the fields, he still saw the fairy lights. This was an excellent sign. Neither he nor Rosea had seen any lights since they traveled back in time. This could mean they were getting their magic back.

Rosea smiled and said, "I am so glad we decided to help the boy's crops tonight."

Looking over back at her was Finn with a considerable smile also. One could see the hope in his eyes that things might get better.

The next day was the weekend's start, and neither worked on the weekends. They usually went to events in the area or learned new things to do. Today was going to be different. Today they were invited to a birthday. Lyreman stated that Aislinn was a dear friend and that her son, Little Anders, would be five today. This was a huge deal! Little Anders was half Fairy; a child could be lost to everyone at five. Aislinn needed all the support and friends she could get. She feared losing her son immensely.

Finn and Rosea had no idea what to buy the little boy. Lyreman stated they must bring a gift for him, which needs to be wrapped and have a big bow on it! The two knew about birthdays, but they never gave gifts on them. They usually made cakes or biscuits and had tea with everyone as a celebration. They lived in the enchanted size for a long time, so celebrating a birthday wasn't a big issue. Some magical people had no idea how old they were. Some were hundreds of years old and still looked young. Not Aislinn, she was beautiful, but she became human to marry a man. Her husband Anders never acquired any magical abilities from marrying her. Aislinn hoped this was a sign that her little boy wouldn't have to disappear into the fairy dream world. Usually, boys lucked out because of how things worked, but every so often. A little boy would vanish, and everyone but a select few would forget him.

Lyreman was one of those few people. It was a burden for him, but he knew it had to happen. It was about balance. For them to know Aislinn and Anders away from the restaurant, Lyreman put Rosea and Finn in charge of the party. They would have it at their cottage since most of the restoration work had been done. Lyreman was proud of what they did but didn't tell them that. Because they were going to have a surprise housewarming party while Little Anders was having his birthday party! Lyreman was slick like that. Rosea and Finn didn't know how to respond to receiving housewarming gifts. This was all new to them, but they quickly realized they liked receiving gifts.

The farmer boy and the girl that lived near him were invited. They showed up first, and Lyreman stepped in behind them since The Butler picked them up also. After Lyreman put a few small wrapped gifts on the table and handed an electric iron to Rosea and a rake to Finn, he stepped back to smoke his pipe and watched their faces. He then met up with Anders, the restaurant owner, who was standing in the backyard taking in the scenery and trying to not think about how his son was turning five.

As more and more people came over, Finn and Rosea got concerned. They had plenty of food and drink. The cake was very nice. It wasn't that. They realized that every gift placed on the table that was for Little Anders was small. Theirs was very large in comparison.

"That is very unique wrapping paper. I really like that. Where did you find that?" Aislinn said, admiring the fabric used to wrap Finn and Rosea's gift. The material created a draped bow on the top.

"Thank you so much, Aislinn. We are new at this. I am sure Lyreman told you of our situation. I just hope Little Anders likes what we picked out for him. We stopped at an antique store and saw something that seemed like a good gift for him. The wrapping is a few antique scarfs. We figured you could use them once Little Anders unwrapped his gift. We have noticed how you sometimes like wearing them to hold up your hair. Seeing all these smaller gifts, we should have gone to the toy store and got a traditional gift." Rosea stated.

"Nonsense, I am sure whatever it is, he will like it. Little Anders likes most things. He sometimes reminds me of an adult and is very inquisitive for his age. Hopefully, we all get to remember him a lot longer. He should be safe if he makes it a few days past his fifth birthday. Although he wouldn't suffer, nor will we, if he vanishes. Since we could all forget him, that's how it's supposed to be. It's just hard to think he could just disappear. And do not take it personally if after Little Anders thanks you for your gift, he says we gave it to him. He thinks that for every gift he gets, we make those people bring them. I am not sure why he believes that. It concerns me. Since it seems like the Dream World is fogging his mind and preparing to take him. But he only considers different things being from us. Simple toys he never thinks we got it for him. We have tried correcting him, but he insists that we got him certain things others gave him." Aislinn stated, looking very concerned.

Finn walked out back to see what everyone was doing. The children were all running in the wheat field chasing butterflies and grasshoppers.

Finn stepped up to Lyreman and took him off to the side, away from others, and asked him, "How come the Farmer's boy doesn't remember me? I was just small when I gave him wishes. I look the same. He doesn't seem to remember me."

Lyreman smiled, "Well, Finn, you look different to him. It is like camouflage. If you were in your Leprechaun size, he would realize who you are. In human form, many of us just look different to humans. I guess it's to hide us among them. I have always wondered if they don't see how I really look. What do they see?"

Lyreman waved everyone in the fields to come in. As they entered, the children gathered around for the party. Finn tried to hold back a chuckle when Little Anders was supposed to wish before blowing out his candle. He couldn't see the purpose of wishing if you would not get that. He found some human traditions funny. After the cake was handed out, Little Anders started to tear into his presents. Dawn was there picking up the paper carnage. She did not like them messing up her clean work. And although well-behaved, Lyreman watched her, ensuring she didn't go off the rail.

Every gift was a small toy, as Finn guessed. Even the little farm boy gave him a small toy. It was an old metal toy tractor the boy had repainted red. Little Anders had no idea it was a used toy. He was happy to have a red tractor to play with. The most significant gift was left for last. When Little Anders removed the scarfs wrapped around it, an ancient wooden box with brass hinges and a brass clasp stood. Anders stepped forward and helped Little Anders open it. Inside was a very lovely old brass microscope. It had slides and some old reagent bottles that still had chemicals. Everyone was surprised at the gift. They all made comments about how nice the gift was.

"I am sorry if it isn't appropriate. We were not sure what to get Little Anders." Finn said, looking over to his wife.

Aislinn was all smiles, "No need to apologize. Little Anders's Dad will enjoy showing his son how to use that. Those two are like two peas in a pod. They usually walk around in the woods just picking stuff to look at. I think this is the perfect gift. They can now look even closer."

Rosea was all smiles, "Well, that's a relief. We bought it because it looked neat and the store owner said children like microscopes. We were unsure if that was true or if he just wanted to sell us something. We don't have children yet, so this is all new to us."

Everyone chuckled, and Lyreman said, "I bet you got Sam. He sometimes helps at the antique shop and is a pretty good salesperson. I am surprised he didn't sell you more stuff."

"Obviously, you know Sam well." Finn continued, "He advised the scarfs as wrapping paper, which worked in Aislinn's favor. He also sold me a few items for our cottage. When I got home, I couldn't believe the stuff I bought that I didn't need! They are nice items, but I didn't need them. Rosea has picked on me since I bought that stuff. Says she will donate them to the burn pile out back. Honestly, I don't think they are that bad."

At this point, all the kids were outside playing with Little Anders and his toys.

Anders senior carried the microscope out to their car. He didn't want the children playing with this without supervision. He planned to use this with Little Anders at the family's orchid grove.

The party went well, and Finn and Rosea gathered many housewarming gifts from those who visited. This included towels for their kitchen, a few bottles of honey wine, jams, and other assorted home preserves. Plus, there were a few kitchen gadgets they had no idea how to use.

Chapter Eight

STRANDED

A few years had gone by. And Finn had given up on getting back to his time. He still couldn't visit his family since the younger version of himself was always around. Although Finn missed home and knew it was better to keep his distance. Rosea knew he was sad at times but didn't push it. She blamed herself. She knew it was her that caused this. They could only time travel if she made it happen. All she understood was they had traveled back to where he was younger, and she was just a Fairy.

"I am truly sorry, My Love," Rosea told Finn as he tried to repair the wall clock that wouldn't wind up.

"Whatever for dear?" Finn asked.

"I am sorry you can not visit your family, and we have never had children. I feel I am to blame for both." Rosea said as she hugged Finn from behind.

Finn didn't seem sad but was somber as he said, "It is not a problem at all. It definitely isn't your fault. I realized that if we had not gone back in time, the land I grew up on would have died. Those I know would have left the area, and my home would have been destroyed. If I don't see my parents till the day we left, about another 15 or more years, which I am guessing by the age of the Farmer's son. I am fine. My Mom doesn't even miss me. My younger self is still with everyone there. At the point when we vanished from our wedding is when we can return.

For us, it will have been years. But for them, it will be like we never left. They might remember us vanishing or something. That's all that would happen. And I have never blamed you. This unwanted trip here fixed the land and saved that farm. Without that, I might have never met you later. You did us both a favor. Plus, you are my family. Lyreman and everyone here have treated us like one of them. We are doing just fine. Even though I would like some more magic ability instead of depending on Lyreman all the time for help."

What Finn said was convincing despite him missing his friends and family. He didn't blame Rosea or want her to worry. So Finn told her what she needed to hear. He wouldn't share with Rosea that he had an ominous feeling that the time-traveling thing wasn't over. So, he focused on being happy to be with her in their current situation.

Finn had gotten very good at fixing thatched roofs. Although he fell through a few in the past years. Repairing roofs was now his skill set. He learned how to do many things from the two boys Lyreman and The Butler brought in to help him with his roof. The two boys, Coilin and Faolan, were mostly farmhands at two different farms. Lyreman had set them on the path of cottage restoration so they could save money and eventually own their own farms. So, Finn learned a lot. The boys seemed to finish each other's sentences, but that oddness was nothing if one considered their work quality and how fast they did it. Finn was grateful.

They even helped him restore an old panel truck to haul supplies in. It was a deep purplish blue color with "FINN'S THATCHERY AND COTTAGE REPAIR" in gold letters on the side of it. Finn had crops of just reed and thatch that he grew for his own use, but he also had a small shop where he processed it for others to use. He could have been better at cottage repair, but he always had help from The Butler or Dawn if needed.

Finn was very popular since he figured out how to keep the lower levels of thatch from rotting on cottage roofs. People only had to change the top layers if they wanted it to look nice. He put a plastic layer down before the final thatch layer. This reduced water dripping inside from the rain like in the past. Some houses were returning to thatch roofs since what Finn was doing worked so well. He didn't like plastic because it wasn't a natural item, but he realized it saved people lots of money. It also allowed one to service their roofs often and only charge a small amount each time.

Mostly, he never let on that the reed and thatch were grown using Leprechaun magic, which made them very attractive. They lasted longer, and enchanted roofs positively affected those living in the houses under them.

Rosea was doing OK but wasn't sure she wanted to keep working in the restaurant. The place was fun to work at because Aislinn made many things about the restaurant experience pleasant for workers besides caring for the customers.

Considering it was not very pricey. The restaurant was very nice. The customers always dressed up to eat there, and most of the profits returned to the dining experience. Even if a person just ordered a burger, they received it in style.

Rosea wanted to quit and desired more from her daily work. But Rosea didn't know what else she could do. Her thoughts about working with Finn concerned her. Finn had once stated that his method was madness but had to happen, or he wouldn't be successful. Oddly, Rosea wanted to avoid success. She just wanted a simple life and didn't wish to ruin Finn's enjoyment of his work. She would have been fine living in a tree with Finn and fixing him acorn soup. But she did love their cottage. It was one of the best looking around since Finn made sure their place was a model home he could use as an advertisement. Finn wasn't trying to be rich. He really liked being good at something. That was what made him happy. He said it was like working with his Dad to make the tools used to harvest acorns.

No sooner as Rosea thought about how she didn't want to work in the restaurant, Aislinn walked in. Rosea was stirring the sauces as usual. Something she had done for the last few years. It never changed. If she wasn't doing that, it was rolling silverware. And at times, she helped seat customers.

Aislinn had a kitchen hand take over what Rosea was doing. They walked outside, and both sat on the brass bench in front of the main window.

"Rosea, I know this isn't the job you really want. We wanted you to have interaction with people. That's a hard thing to learn for some of us. I really struggled when I became human. That is the only reason we wanted you here. Are you unhappy?" Aislinn asked

Rosea was surprised at how quickly the situation changed, and she only thought about leaving as she responded, "I am not unhappy, but I doubt that I wanted to do this. I like people and think I have improved at interacting with them. I honestly have no idea what I would do if I didn't work here."

"Don't worry, Rosea. I know you are a Time Fairy. It must be tough being stuck in a time and unable to leave at will." Aislinn said this, took one of Rosea's hands, held it, and continued, "Don't worry. Just go home early today. We will be fine without you. Meet me here tomorrow wearing jeans and a shirt you don't mind getting dirty. I think I know of something you might enjoy and could make money at."

Rosea met up with Aislinn the following day. They both hopped into Aislinn's old pickup and headed out of town. After driving for a few hours, taking a turn, and then going a few more minutes, they came to a farm with many trees around it and many greenhouse grow tunnels. The long white tunnels had fans on the ends to control their heat and create air movement. Rosea saw a small stream with slow-moving water passing by the tunnels as they drove closer. Pulling up to the farmhouse, a small, petite lady was there to meet them. Aislinn introduced Rosea, and they all walked to the tunnels. They entered into one of them. It was warm and humid inside. A bright light came through the white domed plastic roof that went on for a very long way. On both sides of the walkway down the middle were many orchids, with fans generating a light, slow-moving breeze.

Aislinn looked at Rosea and said, "My friend Tiffany, right here, owns all these greenhouse tunnels. She specializes in many tropical plants and has agreed to show you how to reproduce orchids. It isn't as easy as just collecting seeds and growing more plants. Orchids are difficult to reproduce, but you enjoy working with flowers since you are a Fairy at heart. It's challenging, and hopefully, you can help save our family's orchid grove. The flowers there were planted by Anders's family many generations ago. They brought them back from The States, and have been the family's treasure growing under the grove of trees for generations. And for some odd reason, I feel connected to that area, and it saddens me to see it dying. They are struggling and dying off now. With Tiffany's help, I hope you can figure out what's wrong and fix it."

"Yes. I definitely want to do this. It is very far from home, though." Rosea said, slightly concerned she might not like spending five hours a day driving for work.

Laughing, Tiffany said, "Oh no. I wouldn't do that either. I have spare rooms in my house. You only need to work two or three days during the week here. You can drive here on Monday and return in the evening on Wednesday or Thursday morning. I had to locate here because of the water stream. Since I use lots of water, most of which goes back into the stream without any chemicals. Orchids need thick, humid air movement to thrive. I am sorry if this offer is not appealing. I just had to set up here. And mostly, many people don't want these tunnels near their homes."

"I am sure I can do this. Finn will understand. He would probably schedule his big projects when I was not around. I will talk to him, but we can do this. I also have an old car I can use until we get a better one. How soon can I start." Rosea said as she looked at Tiffany and Aislinn.

Finn was pleased about Rosea getting a different job. He knew she had more to give than just stirring pots. Plus, she loved flowers. She is a Fairy, or at least she was. Tending flowers is what she once did. He also did exactly what Rosea figured he would. Finn started scheduling his big jobs that took all day when she wasn't around. He could fend for himself, and Dawn would help with food if he needed help, but he figured he would just eat a sandwich, which he had grown fond of. A peanut butter and grape jelly sandwich was a favorite. He didn't have either growing up. Dawn showed him how to mix a little honey into the peanut butter to make it extra tasty. Toasting the bread and buttering with salted butter on the inside of the bread also helped the flavor. Finn was amazed at how much he liked human food. Even Rosea enjoyed those sandwiches that one could not eat without having sticky hands afterward. So Finn always packed her one wrapped in wax paper for her trip to the tunnels.

A House Fairy was handy. Which Finn really missed. Since their cottage was in good order, Dawn seldom visited. She lived in Lyreman's cottage, and that was her home. Although she sometimes called Lyreman her Grandfather, Lyreman stated that she was twice as old as him. But if it made her happy to consider him her family. He wasn't going to correct her. So. Sandwiches would have to do, and Finn needed the honey in them to use his Leprechaun magic. But the peanut butter and grape jelly were imported, and Finn could not buy them locally. He never asked for it, but The Butler occasionally dropped off a few jars and other items.

One day, also included in the box of goods was a glass bottle of imported pancake syrup in the shape of a lady. It had a note telling him to add it to the peanut butter instead of honey for when he didn't need enchantment magic. Finn was always surprised at how The Butler treated him like a friend or son. And since he couldn't visit his family and friends, this mattered a lot.

After a few weeks, Rosea had gotten very good at caring for Tiffany's orchids in the tunnels. She started learning how to propagate orchids, although it was tricky. There was a particular room that was sterile and temperature-controlled. Rosea couldn't use magic like she once did as a Fairy to get the flowers to reproduce. Instead, she used sterilized glass Erlenmeyer flasks to cultivate the orchid sprouts. Then, the flasks had to be carefully broken to remove the tiny new orchids. Each flask could sprout a few hundred new plants. Rosea had gotten very good at this.

Finn got used to coming home sometimes and seeing a new orchid near a window getting bright indirect light since the flowers didn't like direct sunlight. And the flowers did remind him of living in the woods he grew up in. Then, one day, a small pot with a slight pinkish orchid was in the middle of the kitchen table. It was unique compared to the others Rosea had brought home, which usually had larger flowers.

"What is this one?" Finn asked Rosea.

"That represents why Aislinn had me work for her friend Tiffany at her orchid tunnels. Anders Sr.'s family has a private orchid grove a little ways down the road. It is many generations old. That little orchid is known as a fairy slipper orchid. The grove was once covered with these, but something started to kill them off. I have started reproducing them at the tunnels, but I don't know why the ones at the grove are dying now." Rosea said, sounding like she lacked confidence she could do this.

Finn hugged her and stated, "You've got this. I know you. If you can get a corn shaker like me to marry you. You can do this... Can we visit this area where they grow? I mean. Can I go there?"

"Sure. Aislinn wouldn't mind. Maybe you can help me figure out something I have not noticed. Your ability to grow the best reed and thatch materials came from reading and talking to the surrounding farmers. You might have picked up on something helpful." Rosea stated as she sat down. She had just returned from working out of town and was tired from the long drive.

The next few days, Finn made sure to eat anything with honey in it, and he also gathered local brook water and filtered it, which he made tea with. He did this without letting Rosea know and let her think he was working. Finn didn't have any pending jobs but instead went to a local library and then stopped to talk to the lady who lived by The Farmer's son. She grew regular flowers, and he usually brought items to give to her, like bread, sugar, and milk, to thank her for whatever advice she had.

Today, there was a small pack of cookies in the simple grocery gift, and the little girl quickly asked for them and ran off after being handed the small package. Most probably to share with the little boy. Finn didn't have any luck getting any information from the lady. She knew nothing about orchids but said most plants share similar requirements. Stating that orchids were no different. Although they might have different light, water, air, soil, and fertilizer requirements, they still had them. She stated that Finn needed to figure those out. Only then would he fix the problem.

Finn returned to the library and found a reference to orchids and their requirements. His only practical knowledge was planting his reeds and thatch, which grew. Just some creek water and they succeeded without any effort from him. And they did exceptionally well, and when he enchanted them, it was as if they would double in size overnight. So he needed to be more knowledgeable because if his wife Rosea and Tiffany could not figure it out. How was he going to help? Finn found one book that mentioned orchid reproduction and wasn't a typical library book but a pamphlet that looked more like a training aid for a new hire at an orchid farm. It had a few paragraphs about the seeds and explained how fungus was required. He wasn't sure what would help this particular type of orchid. Because there seemed to be different rules for many different varieties. And no book he read ever showed the variety his wife brought home. This pamphlet was the only information that contained more details about orchid cultivation besides primary house plant care. And it only had twenty pages. So he read it a few times. But still, none of the pictures resembled the flower his wife was trying to save.

Rosea had been cooking and decorating. Finn entered the house with a few books he had checked out from the library.

"Are you ready for our Saturday trip?" Rosea said as Finn tried not to drop the stack of books he entered with.

Finn smiled and let some books do a controlled fall on the table, "Yes, I am. Let's hope we figure it out."

Finn had a big grin. He was as positive as possible. He knew Rosea wanted this to go well. She desired to always be in charge of keeping that grove alive. She figured if she could do that, it would prove that she had worth and hopefully get her own flower tunnels to grow flowers, herbs, or tropical plants. She had heard many grew small cherry trees in them, which was the best way to grow many things in the local weather.

She had hopes and dreams. What she didn't know was that Finn knew this. He knew she needed this success.

She was loved and valued by him, but she required personal success. Since they couldn't have children from what they started to suspect, he knew these orchids represented something she needed. That's why he ate more honey and drank more creek water than he had ever done before. But he avoided drinking cow's milk since the cows ate clover. And that would trigger his enchanted magic before he was ready.

Chapter Nine

FAIRY ORCHIDS

THE following day, Finn and Rosea hopped into that old beat-up car. Since a person working for Finn needed to use his panel truck. Rosea had packed a light lunch and her tools and supplies in case they needed them. Finn had grabbed a handful of clover and put it in his pocket. He had a patch near the main gate for that purpose. But made sure Rosea was not paying attention when he did this.

Rosea said to Finn while driving, "I saw that! I know what you are up to, you sly dog. Enchantment will not help because every test says the soil is perfect. But any help will be appreciated at this point because I have lost hope we can save this orchid grove."

Finn just smiled. He was sure they would figure it out. If they couldn't find a solution, eating several clover leaves in his pocket might do the trick. It wouldn't be pretty, but he was sure he would have so much enchanting power that the orchids had to do better.

When they arrived, they set up a picnic in the middle under the surrounding grove's trees. Only a tiny clump of orchids grew on one side of the area. Under, the circle of trees looked empty, with only a large area of humus soil that was soft to walk on. Even while she took care of them, she saw many plants die. Several had tried to help Aislinn save her family's secret garden patch of fairy slipper orchids. They all had theories, but no one had any luck fixing the diminishing crop of once-over-abundant orchids that at one time were so thick they overlapped and bunched under that shaded canopy.

While they ate their lunch, Finn asked item after item, trying to see if what he learned could help.

Finn asked, "Light?"

Rosea, "Nope, we removed any branches that blocked too much light. These orchids love bright, indirect light. This area gets that in the morning and the late evening. The tree's canopy blocks the brutal midday sun. Too much sun, and the orchids burn as if they are vampires. They hate the midday sun."

Finn said, "That's nice to know. How about the wind? Don't these need more air movement to spread the pollen?"

"That is a great idea, and we looked into that. We have been hand-pollinating, but the plants just keep dying. No new seeds seem to be germinating.", Rosea said in a disheartening manner.

"I know. I saw how the still-existing flowers seemed on one end, as if the blowing wind had pollinated them. I am guessing those plants must be downwind and the last to get pollinated and reproduce. They are probably the last plants to grow and hit maturity before this problem started. So that could be why they are the last ones dying." Finn said, knowing he was grasping at straws.

While they sat there looking over at the remaining few orchids. Finn noticed a ladybug walking across the top of the picnic basket's handle. He reached down and let it walk onto his hand. He figured they picked it up during their walk from the car.

Finn held out his hand and said. "I think I know. Well, I have part of it. I still have a few more ideas, but I know part of it."

Rosea looked at Finn, observing the ladybug, "Finn, those don't pollinate. They eat bad bugs. How is a ladybug a fix?"

"Rosea, I have read a lot in the past few days. I let you rest while I went to the library and then visited a few farmers. The organic ones seemed to tell me things I never even considered. They said things that make me wonder. So hear me out. It just occurred to me." Finn paused and finally continued, "I have not seen one bug since we have been here. Not a one! This ladybug is the first. And that is only because it came in on our basket."

Finn had Rosea's attention. You could see her interest. She never thought about no bugs. They are needed to pollinate. Then she spoke up, "Finn, even if that is so. We hand pollinate. Why are the seeds not growing?"

Finn was all grins. He was sure he had this. So he stated what he was told, "Rosea, I was told that all plants are the same and need the same things to live and thrive but in different quantities. I think that isn't so for these particular flowers. They have special requirements, and the bugs are just part of it."

Finn continued and asked, "Does this soil have fungus?"

"Yes," said Rosea, "It has mycelium threads if you pull back the soil. Orchids need fungus to hatch the seeds, and we have checked to see if that was missing. Orchid seeds have no food source in them like most seeds. The fungus transports the soil nutrients into them, and then the fungus feeds off the roots. It's a relationship they both benefit from.

"I agree. I heard many organic farmers say that fungus was essential. I even read this in an obscure orchid pamphlet. What my real question is: Is it the right kind of fungus? Can the wrong fungus grow?" Finn asked.

Rosea had a very blank stare on her face. She couldn't believe what she was hearing. It sounded like Finn came up with something they never questioned. They figured that the fungus growing was the correct one. They never saw the plants infected by a fungus that made them rot. The bad funguses usually did that.

So Rosea spoke up, "That might be it, Finn. I do not think anyone questioned that. I was always told the fungus was present, and no rot fungus was ever noticed. No one ever questioned if the right type was growing. The adult orchid plants don't need the fungus, but what if they don't reproduce well without the right fungus? The seeds need the right fungus to hatch and grow. The lack of insects is a huge issue with everything in bloom. We never saw one insect fly in here. These orchids mostly need bees, but any insect can help."

Finn held out hope. He was curious to know if he was even remotely correct. Finn had a hunch and hoped it was accurate for his wife's sake. He needed it to be right because he knew she needed this. All of a sudden, Rosea stated that she would be right back and headed towards the car. She returned with her work bag, pulled back soil around one of the plants, and took a sample near its roots. She repeated this on a few more plants. She worked with excitement. Finn had no answer, but he made her question something else. He figured he was partially correct on a few things. And hopefully, it would be what she needed to figure this out. Rosea took Finn's hand and walked him out one side of the grove, and they were looking at a cornfield.

Pointing at the field, Rosea said excitedly, "That's it! That's the reason. I believe the good fungus is dead or struggling. They most probably spray this corn crop with a fungicide. The plane probably finishes its run past the edge of the field, and this grove is at that edge. That could be it!"

Finn just looked at her, held out a handful of wilted clover he pulled from his pocket, and said, "So I guess I don't need to eat this? With a smirk on his face."

"Oh, You're eating that! You will eat that, go back into that grove, and enchant that orchid soil like you never enchanted before!" Rosea said, looking at Finn seriously as he stood there with his mouth open in shock at her comment. He wanted to laugh because it was funny, but he knew she meant it.

On the way home, Finn had Rosea drive again because he was still a Leprechaun and waited for his human size to kick in. So they would stay out of town and not stop for anything or anyone. Finn was worried it might take a long time to become human again after eating a large quantity of the things that make enchanted soil. He feared they might have to visit Lyreman, who made it so Finn could still enchant the crops because he overdid it this time. It was getting dark, and they arrived at their cottage. Finn was still tiny. Rosea chuckled at him. She picked him up against his will and carried him inside the cottage. He was not amused. As Rosea got ready for sleep, Finn was still tiny. The bed was so high that Rosea had to lift him up into it.

She pulled back the sheets and asked, "Do you need me to tuck you in?" As she stood there with a smile going from ear to ear.

"Not funny, Love. This reminds me of when you tossed all that water on me. Yes. I'm having flashbacks!" Finn said with a smirk on his face.

He knew it was funny. He was still wearing his clothes and shoes. Finn didn't have little people pajamas, and he worried that his shoes would not get bigger if he took them off and became human. Liking his shoes and the clothes, he kept it all on. He figured Rosea would have said something persnickety about him wearing dirty clothes to bed, but she didn't.

Then, as the lights went off, and they started to drift off to sleep, Rosea said, "Oh, you are changing the sheets when you become full size again. Who actually wears shoes to bed?"

Finn could hear Rosea lightly laughing as he finally drifted to sleep.

Chapter Ten

FUNGUS

MONDAY could not happen fast enough. Rosea headed to Tiffany's tunnel farm. Since Finn returned to his standard size again, she felt she needed to head to work. Tiffany and Rosea tested some of the soil. They showed the correct fungus was present. So, Rosea was a little let down hearing that.

Then Tiffany stated, "Until now, I never questioned the test. I just assumed the fungus was alive since it turned the solution in the test tube the correct color. It wasn't very dark blue like it was supposed to be, but it was blue, meaning the correct fungus was there. We see this light color all the time in new growth samples. These are old growth samples. It should be dark blue. We just always knew fungus was there. You have me questioning this whole thing."

"What do you mean? Is the fungus dead? Shouldn't it have disappeared if it died?" Rosea said with a concerned look.

Tiffany said, "No. Well, I don't know. This is new to me. That soil has been tested by many of us. We never questioned it, but you said the cornfield is probably crop-dusted with a fungicide. And since most farms in this area are organic, it is most likely a natural fungicide. Synthetic fungicide makes the good fungus grow well since it is engineered only to hurt the harmful fungus. A natural fungicide does not play favorites. It kills all fungi, even the good ones. The fungus is trying to grow but is too weak to grow at the top of the organic compost in the grove. The soil must be very contaminated on top. That's where the seeds fall. No seeds can hatch and grow without the fungus being in the top layer of soil."

Rosea knew there was hope and asked, "Where do we go from here?"

Tiffany stated, "First, you must go and collect samples from the top layer of soil near the plants at the grove. Try and get some from an area that was never disturbed. Also, collect soil from the orchid sprouts we grew in the tunnels. This could also explain why we could grow the orchids from seed here using our beakers, and any plant we put in the grove from the tunnels died fast. It wasn't old enough to endure the lack of fungus in the soil. And young plants need fungus to develop and mature."

"Is that all? Just get topsoil samples?" Rosea asked, looking confused.

"That's just the beginning. Please ask Finn if he knows who owns that farm and have him explain to them what's going on. Please have the farmer call me. I will tell him what fungicide is safe for his crops and our orchids in the grove. I am sure I can help the farmer get the safe chemical cheaper than he is getting the natural stuff. Sometimes, organic isn't good if it kills everything else! This would explain why we no longer saw mushrooms in the grove like we once did. So please ask this favor of Finn. We will figure this out. I will drive the samples to a friend who will test for the fungicides and tell me if the good fungus is dead. So as soon as you get back, I will take all the samples to my friend. If you drop them off at night on my porch, that is OK. Just go back home. I will call when I get back. My brother can come by and watch the tunnels for me. I have recently kept him away because he is so set in his ways. But he means well." Tiffany said.

Rosea said, "Are you sure? I can help you if needed. I am sure Finn would understand. Plus, he is OK staying here and helping me if he doesn't have work scheduled."

Tiffany said, "I need you to talk to Aislinn and tell her what we are doing. Try and get her to get involved with the farmer spraying his crops, and also, you need to see if they are spraying any pesticides. You stated how you never see any bugs there. Suppose that ladybug came from home with you. That could mean the bugs are not even pollinating. The corn crops can be pollinated by the wind. Actually, any insect pollinates them. Even flies! Fairy slipper orchids need bees to pollinate them, and they need the stupid young bees. The older bees won't go near an orchid. They know that it's a fruitless trip. The orchid smells sweet, and the color is inviting, but the young bee goes and finds nothing. There is no nectar or pollen they can collect. They visit a few more flowers, and that's how the orchid gets pollinated. The bee quickly learns as he gets older to stay away from the orchids. And there are always more young bees since they usually do not live longer than thirty days. So there are always plenty of young bees who don't know an orchid is a waste of their time.

We are lucky that one of these orchid flowers can produce countless thousands of seeds at a time. So, the fact those plants are not making any new plants in the grove is incredible. Finn was right about those remaining orchids. They are probably dying from old age. The rest also died for the same reason. We need bees and no fungicide. You do that, and I will get the test done. You figured it out. You and Finn have excellent intuition. The two of you are definitely a good team. What you two have done is nothing short of magical. Many people have tried to figure this out. Aislinn has helped multitudes of people over the years. This is the least we can do for her because this grove has an emotional connection to her that is above average. It would be like losing a family member."

Rosea dropped off the soil samples that night and went home. Finn had her ride with him in his "Thatch

Mobile," as Rosea called it, to the corn farmer's house. It was a straightforward conversation, and they gave him one of Tiffany's work cards to call. Being an organic farmer for all the right reasons made this farmer concerned that his organic treatments were killing items in nature; this news upset him and his wife.

They never knew those orchids existed. Finn and Rosea walked with them to the orchid grove and showed them the area. They were amazed at the ample space under the encircling trees, with only a few orchids holding on near one edge of that area. They stated they also used a natural pesticide and would ensure it wasn't ever sprayed on or near the grove area. And promised to apply it from a sprayer on a tractor instead of using a plane like they were using. They only used the aircraft since it was cheaper and were saving for the sprayer they could pull with their tractor. Most importantly, they wouldn't use the sprayer on the last few field rows near the trees. Plus, they would ensure to only spray when a breeze wasn't in the direction of the trees.

Rosea said that this was more than good enough. She also stated that Tiffany would help them get the correct chemicals at a reasonable cost. She wasn't sure but noted that the lack of good fungus might have weakened their crops. She explained how the roots needed good fungus and how a synthetic fungicide was sometimes safer and might not impact their organic license.

Finn and Rosea headed home, and while driving home, Finn said, "That was great. You really are on your way to fixing this. I honestly didn't know anything when I was asking questions. I just read a lot and hoped it would help."

Rosea looked at him, "I know you worried about it. I know you. Even if I laugh at you when you're struggling with the smallness. You still love me. Plus, it really did take both of us. I doubt your enchantment will help until the poison is purged from the soil in the area. That will take lots of water and time. If lucky, Tiffany will find chemicals to encourage the correct fungus to grow and help break down the natural fungicide.

Hey, where are you going?"

Finn took a small side road and headed towards an orchard with field after field of apple trees. He just looked at her and smiled. Finn wasn't telling her anything. She tried to get him to talk, but he just kept driving. They pulled up to a small store on the edge of the property and parked.

Finn headed up the wooden stairs into the store. It was nothing spectacular. It was just a roadside shop for the locals to buy the apples grown there. Several varieties were in barrels and in bins. There were even some black apples. Finn could never buy one of those because they seemed dark and ominous. Rosea followed him in and realized this was where Finn had picked up apples to bring home in the past. They were all good. She also realized he never got any black or green apples to bring home. She did recognize the ones that looked like they had stars on them. But the pink ones were her favorites. Those were called Fairies Blush. They were very crisp and lightly sweet. She figured Finn disliked the green ones because they were called Leprechaun Madness. It was just the farmers trying to profit from the local lore of the parts. Then she saw a black variety and was grateful he never brought them home. They looked icky to her. They probably tasted good, but they didn't look right. Not in the least.

"Rosea, I would like you to meet a friend of mine. This is Colin. He was one of the guys who helped me learn my thatching business." Finn said as he shook Colin's hand.

Colin told Finn, "It is so nice for you to revisit me. It's almost twice a week now!" Colin looked at Rosea, winked, and said, "It is very nice to meet you finally, Rosea. We always finished our day's work before you were home. Finn sure does talk a lot about you. So what brings the two of you in today so late in the evening?"

Rosea looked at Finn, wondering the same exact thing. Finn just walked out of the store and stood on its covered porch. He pointed into the distance where several stacks of white boxes with little tin roofs stood near the fence line encrusted with wildflowers beyond the apple trees.

"How do I get some of those?" Finn asked.

"You want bee hives? What in the world would you want that for? You don't need them for growing reed or thatch. That only takes lots of water, good soil, and slightly marshy land. You could get yourself all stung up messing with those little… Oops. Almost forgot my manners. So. Why would you need those?" Colin said as he noticed that Rosea seemed to have a light go off as if she just got the same idea as Finn.

Finn pointed at Rosea and said. "That's right! At the very least, we need one stack for the orchids."

"Wait a minute. Do you need bees for orchids? Why not just use the beaker method?" Colin said, looking at the both of them.

Rosea seemed surprised so many people knew a lot about growing things. Even care for items that she thought were rare seemed common knowledge. So she replied, "You seem to know a lot about plants. What do you know about orchids?"

Colin just laughed, "Not much at all, actually. I only know what my friend Faolan told me. Tiffany is his sister. She owns those orchid tunnels I hear you work at. That's where he is right now. He is your bee guy. I bet he could get you a hive for free. He is always looking for new lands to get different honey from. He says different flowers make different-tasting honey. It's his hobby, but we also get money moving those stacks around to help pollinate the apple trees and other crops. I am here running this store for my girlfriend. I usually help her when I am not tending one of my fields. Her family owns the apple orchards, and her Dad says he will buy our farm a new tractor if we help him sell apples locally. He ships most of his apples to other countries, but he would like to sell them more to people around here. So he built this store. If you wait around long enough, Faolan's girlfriend will show up. She can tell you more about bees than I can."

After talking to Faolan's girlfriend, Finn, and Rosea were happy they visited. They knew enough to get an area ready for the bee hive.

Mostly, they realized that Faolan's girlfriend kept saying, "Don't forget that we are getting married next month. It's a double wedding. Coilin and Faolan have asked me and my best friend to marry them simultaneously."

She stated this so many times they lost track of it. She also informed them that bee hives should not go in the constant direct sun if possible. She insisted that most beekeepers were just plain cruel. They learned that bees naturally built their hives in partially shaded areas and out of the sun. Faolan told her they try to place the hives under trees whenever possible. At least partial shade when available. She stated that many farmers were greedy by trying to ensure the bees did two crops, so they put them at a cleared fence line in the open sun or in the middle of a field.

So many new beekeepers see that the hives are in the full sun, and they do the same. They will even insist that the hives be in the full sun all day even though they don't know why they do this. Finn and Rosea learned the bees needed to be out of the cold wind or direct afternoon sun. It was sometimes OK to place near a fence since the high grass or wildflowers on a fence line stopped the wind and excess sun. However, she kept stressing they should not freeze or cook the bees; placement was the biggest concern. Besides access to a natural water source. Which the grove property had. It was just a tiny stream, but it would be more than adequate. With this information, Finn and Rosea thanked everyone and headed home. Before they were reminded about that double wedding again.

Chapter Eleven

THE PROJECT

A week had passed, and Tiffany was not home yet. She took a more extended trip than Rosea thought she would. So Rosea visited with Aislinn and shared with her the hopefully good news. Aislinn was so happy that she told Rosea to let Faolan and Colin know they could eat at the restaurant for free with their girlfriends. She also said she would buy any honey harvested from that bee hive they put near the grove. She was sure it would sell at the restaurant as Faerie Aislinn honey.

Later in the following week, Tiffany brought a special crew into the grove area, besides digging up all the remaining orchids and transporting them to Tiffany's tunnels for safekeeping. All the soil inside the circle of trees and dirt was removed at least a foot down for several feet past the trees. It was an enormous undertaking. Several dump trucks of earth were removed. Rosea showed up every day and wasn't required to do much. Tiffany kept paying her, saying that this was extremely important to Aislinn. So Rosea just helped out when she could. The farmers who had poisoned the grove while having their crops dusted visited Aislinn and apologized. Aislinn was highly understanding, knowing the farmers were trying to grow healthy foods using natural items. And she didn't blame them. They also became a food source for her restaurant. She had learned they grew unusual garden herbs and vegetables in a small area, which would help make The Faerie Aislinn's menu more interesting.

"How is it going?" Finn asked Rosea when she came home one night.

"Wow. Who would have thought a simple area would need so much work?" Rosea said, sounding exhausted.

"What do you mean, so much work?" Finn asked as he had Rosea sit at the table and gave her a bowl of vegetable beef soup. It was one of her favorites, with or without beef.

Rosea said between bites, "The fungicide that was used must have been dumped as the plane would circle back to do other parts of the crop. They think the crop duster the farmer used must have also dumped the remaining chemicals at the end of the crop so he wouldn't have to deal with disposal if he landed with it. The soil tests showed an enormous level of the fungicide. The good fungus was still alive but just barely. No good fungus was alive at the soil surface for the top few inches. This is where the seeds germinate, and the fungus helps feed them till maturity. So, the soil was toxic and had to be removed. They are bringing in many water trucks to spray the surrounding area and the trees with a special soap solution to help break down the remaining fungicide."

Finn looked bewildered, "Where are they going to get the proper type of soil with the right type of fungus in it? That seems like a lot of soil to replace. Several dump truckloads have driven back and forth from that area."

"Well, that's not so bad. Although the soil was unique under the trees. The cedar needles, bark, and tree leaves created the perfect environment for the fairy orchids' rhizomes. Since orchids don't have roots, the fungus helped feed nutrients to the orchid by breaking down the organic matter and feeding the plants by attaching to those root-like rhizomes. The items that made up the soil created the perfect pH and helped the orchids thrive in the past. The one saving grace is Tiffany has us keep all the old orchid bark and dirt from our work in the tunnels. The vast compost pile behind the work barn looks like a hill. She has almost enough to replace what they dug out. They will mix peat moss that was dried and chopped up from the local bogs to bulk it up and make it closer to this particular orchid's needs." Rosea said

"How long will the good fungus take to grow?" Finn asked.

"Sorry, Dear. That's easy. So much I forgot to say. The fungus grows all on its own. It doesn't need the orchid to grow. The orchid needs it. So, the massive pile of old bark and soil is already colonized with the good stuff. Tiffany said they would transplant the orchids back into the grove once she feels it's established. They will keep bringing water trucks to the area to wash things down with that special soap and help the new soil compost a little before putting plants in it."

"Well, I have talked to Faolan, and he stated that the bee hive will be installed as soon as they stop watering constantly. He will place it on the back side where the hive will get some sun but be shaded during the hottest part of the day. Also, the wind is a lot less in that spot. The flowers on the surrounding rocky hills are a variety that Faolan doesn't have in his honey collection. He also got permission to seed in more native flowers to help the bees since orchids offer nothing the bees can consume. I think you did it. Who would have thought the act of an organic farmer caused all of this?" Finn said, contemplating the situation.

Rosea kindly defended the organic farmers, "In most situations, this would have never happened. The fungicide would have never hurt any other crop. It just happens to hurt orchids and them reproducing. If not for that. Those farmers were actually doing things correctly and being natural about it. I just hope, for Aislinn's sake, this works. She has spent a lot of money doing this. Tiffany has donated her time and all that old soil that was supposed to be used again in her tunnels. Mr. Anders doesn't seem to mind how much is spent fixing the grove. He said that it was irreplaceable and it was Aislinn's most prized possession and only second to her son Little Anders and him."

Finn picked up Rosea's empty bowl and washed it, then stated, "Well. Now that we are done with that. We should ask where has Lyreman and The Butler been this whole time. The last time I saw either one was when all of this started. I can still enchant crops and sneak out at night to help that new soil in the grove. As long as you are there to drive."

"Knock!, Knock!, Knock!..."

Finn looked at Rosea and smiled. He knew saying Lyreman's name would get a response. He didn't figure it would be this soon.

Upon opening the door, Tiffany stood with Aislinn, Anders, and Little Anders. Finn didn't expect that. He figured that Lyreman would show up. Which Lyreman usually did if Finn talked foul of him. But standing at his door were people he visited, and they seldom ever showed up at the cottage.

"Invite our friends in. Don't just stare at them." Rosea said to Finn, who must have been caught in his mind trying to decide what to do. Finn was known to go into shock if caught off guard, which had been happening much more lately.

"I am sorry. I am just surprised to see all of you here this evening. What prompts this visit?" Finn said as he waved everyone in.

Rosea was already getting everyone a drink and preparing a tray of biscuits. Everyone came in and took a seat at the kitchen table. Finn and Rosea didn't own a couch or much else to sit on besides a few old recliners they used by the fireplace. They didn't entertain much.

Aislinn spoke up, "Well, thanks for your hospitality, but we are here to discuss something that involves all of us. Plus, we must tell you why Lyreman made it a big deal since you are here in our town."

Anders looked at his wife, "Continue, Dear. This needs to be said so they understand the importance of this visit."

Tiffany just sat there holding a cloth napkin in her hands. Something was in it, but she never showed it. Finn grabbed a stool to face everyone, and Rosea stood there. She usually never sat when discussing urgent things. Anders showed Little Anders outside and told him he could play but stay near the cottage and away from the creek. Anders came back and sat down.

Aislinn continued, "Finn and Rosea, you both need to know that everyone here in this room except Little Anders knows who the two of you are. We knew who you were before you came to us a few years ago. It might come as a surprise, but Tiffany and I are also from the fairy dream world. We were not born there like the two of you. I lost my natural family and only retained a few memories of them and previous things, unlike Tiffany, who is not an average enchanted person. But we are here because of what was found today that might also help the two of you."

Tiffany removed the napkin to reveal a small gold coin in her hand. It was a nice coin with a small Fairy on one side, and when Tiffany turned it over, it had a Leprechaun on the back. Then Finn reached into his right pocket and pulled out a coin just like it! Rosea knew he kept his lucky gold coin in his pocket, but she never looked at it. Finn always had it in his pocket or his nightstand drawer.

Standing there, Finn asked, "How can you have my coin, and I also have it?"

Lyreman popped into the room and said, "Because it's the same coin."

Finn looked at Lyreman, feeling relieved, and said, "About time you showed up."

"Time, That's the correct term." Lyreman said as he went on, "Tiffany, please put your coin away, and you are to give it to Aislinn later. I will explain this. Finn knows this coin.

He doesn't realize that he placed his coin in an area where we would find it. Tiffany, tell everyone what you found."

Tiffany said, "When the old soil dug from the orchid grove was brought to my farm. I had them dump it far from the stream and away from my crops. I wanted the fungicide to decompose and the soil to become safe eventually. I let my brother and his friend dump old thatch from roof repair to enrich that soil pile. When my brother Faolan was turning the thatch into the soil pile so it could compost, he saw this gold coin. He also noticed something that stood out to him. There were small pieces of wood in that soil. Those pieces of wood had edges, like wood that was once a small box. He gathered lots of what he found. There was also a very corroded piece of a small brass hinge. When he showed what he found, I realized it could be from one of Aislinn's ancestors since they created and cared for that grove."

Rosea looked concerned and asked, "How did that coin get there, and how can it be here twice?"

Lyreman laughed and answered her question, "Rosea, no need to worry. One coin just catches the other one. That's why I had Tiffany put it away. The coins are out of time, meaning they don't belong here. Either one of them. Lyreman held out his hand and asked Finn to put his coin in it."

Lyreman looked the coin over some, handed it back, and continued, "That is quite a unique coin. I am guessing your family gave that to you?"

Finn nodded and said, "My Dad gave this to me one day when he said I needed a starter gold coin for my collection. So he gave me the coin my family handed to him to start his coin collecting. When I have a son, I am supposed to pass it on."

"Well, Finn, you might never pass that coin on. I believe you have had children or will and lost them to the dream world. Being in human form makes your children prone to that. I normally remember children that many forget. But if you look at Aislinn, who is right here, I will tell you she is your child." Lyreman said with a smirk.

Rosea was all smiles. She wanted a little girl, but Aislinn was older than her. She didn't remember anything about having a child. Finn was in shock. He was a Dad and never knew it.

Lyreman elaborated more, "Aislinn wasn't just born here. I do not believe Finn and Rosea have yet to have a child and lost it already. I think they went back in time. Do either of you own a small wooded box with brass hinges?"

Finn walked into another room, returned with a small box with brass hinges and clasp, and asked, "Like this one I bought at the antique store?"

"That's it!" Tiffany said, "That's the same shape those hinges had. They were fancy like that."

Anders stated. "That grove has been in my family for generations. They planted that with flowers they brought back from their travels. The story was that it once had a tiny cottage. I understand many small stones outside the tree circle were once inside the grove. They were said to be part of the cottage. This land has great value to my history. When Aislinn wanted to marry in the grove, the orchids were prolific. I was impressed that she wanted to honor my family's ties to this land by marrying there. Now it looks like. The land was originally Aislinn's and could be why she is so attached to it."

"Anders, I am sure you are correct. Your Aislinn must have been born near that old cottage spot and disappeared into the fairy dream world. She has such a large affinity for that area. Finn and Rosea must have also visited that place where they had Aislinn. The trees must have grown around the cottage area, so they encircle an empty area in the middle. I believe Finn left that coin on purpose. It's because we talked about it, or he left it, so we eventually find it because gold doesn't decay. He might not have known that coin would be found, but he held out hope. I believe that coin was buried for a reason and that Aislinn needs to hold onto it." Lyreman said.

"What do we do now, Lyreman? I can't travel, and Finn can't use magic or change his size unless you help him." Rosea said, looking stressed.

Tiffany spoke up, "That is easy. It will happen sooner or later. It already has since we found this coin. I am part Fairy, and my brother has no magic. Faolan doesn't believe in Fairies or Leprechauns at all. He has no idea his Mom was a Fairy and that his future wife shows signs of magic. He is such a non-believer we can't bring up the magical world in any form. I am lucky that I did not go into the fairy dream world all the way. I never wanted to marry, which probably spared me the horror of disappearing. Faolan just has no magic. I am sure the dream world really just didn't want him. I love my brother to death, but he has a lot of hate for the traditions we have. I can move between the fairy realms and the human realm easily. I also can keep some memories others forget. This is why I have told Lyreman that I don't remember you two ever having a child, and Lyreman is too close to you to remember some items at times."

Aislinn stood up, "We should go. I see that Finn and Rosea need to process this."

Everyone headed out. Lyreman waited a few minutes, and the Rolls showed up. Before getting into the car, he told

Finn and Rosea, "I believe the two of you are stranded in our time to help. When that help is done, you both will move elsewhere. Only a little is known about Time Fairies since they are so rare, but I am positive both of you get your magic back and can travel when and where you want." Lyreman seemed confident as he stated this. It was as if he knew something. He always knew something. But he only sometimes shared that info.

His name was Lyreman, and that was what everyone called him. But it was not his actual name. No one knew his real name. He took that name on. After all, he was called Liar Man in the distant past because he got caught lying often. It wasn't that he meant anyone harm or was trying to deceive them. His lies were designed to protect a person from things that might harm them. However, he wasn't good at lying hundreds of years ago. But he had gotten much better over the ages.

Even with ages of practice, many enchanted people know when he withholds information. They can feel it. But humans are clueless except for a select few whose spirits once existed in the fairy realm. And this is the way it is supposed to be.

Chapter Twelve

ENDLESS RAIN

IT rained for days. If it didn't rain one day, it was still cloudy and rained the day after. This went on for a whole month. Finn kept checking his pocket to see if his gold coin was there, wondering what the grove had to do with it.

On the other hand, Rosea was pleased since the excessive rain would help the area. Flushing the area of toxins and making it safer to plant the orchids they had temporarily growing in the tunnels. Which was a challenge on its own. The calypso fairy slipper orchid was almost impossible to propagate or grow in captivity, and even the most experienced growers would only attempt to grow them in nature. So, the sooner the area was safe to use, the better.

Due to the plentiful rainfall and perfect soil tests, the orchids were eventually planted in the grove. Aislinn visited the site with Rosea and Finn often. Even though no one remembered the other from the past, they became good friends. Rosea figured that if she were to enjoy the presence of her daughter, she would do her best while the opportunity was there. Finn also did his best to interact with Aislinn. Her being older than them and their child was sometimes strange for him. Aislinn overlooked the issue. It seemed natural for her the way things were virtually upside down. Tiffany also visited often, and Rosea no longer worked for her.

Taking care of the grove and helping Finn with his company was all Rosea cared to do. They didn't need much, and she and Finn figured that they would travel back in time again at any point. That found coin was proof of this. Finn still had his gold coin, and he knew Aislinn had the one they acquired from the orchid grove. Finn did try to hide his concern. He didn't think he would see his parents again or his friends. The fact his coin was found after being left in the past only pushed him further away. Even if enchanted people lived in the time they went. They could only interact with a few. They might ruin the future. And this was one thing Finn was struggling with. His Mom and Dad were down the road a few hours, but he could never visit them. His poor Mom knew he existed but was required to never talk about it since she saw Finn's younger self daily.

One day, Lyreman showed up and asked Rosea and Finn to get inside his Rolls. He asked Finn to get his little wooden box, and they climbed into the back of the car with him. Lyreman seemed almost hesitant but also eager to show them something.

"O.K. Lyreman, Why the mystery? You always hide stuff from us. What is going on now." Finn said, worried that Lyreman had been holding out on information again.

"Don't worry. I am sure that both of you will be fine. We have to try something today. I got a visit today from Rosea." Lyreman said.

Both Finn and Rosea had the look of shock on their faces.

Rosea said, "I don't remember visiting you. Was it a future me?"

Lyreman smiled and said, "Yes. Yes, it was." The little man seemed totally fine with the news he was relaying. So he continued, "Rosea visited me and told me what she needed to do. Why I have hidden this from both of you is because I have known the two of you for hundreds of years. You don't remember me, but I was introduced to you two after this timeline. I have had to hide the truth from you. Anything I knew might have stopped you from doing what the enchanted realm needed. We have no control over what it wants, but it usually gives us what we need. Aislinn, at some point, is taken from you, and you at least were able to get to know her for a short time. I believe that was only part of your purpose here. The son of that farmer and Finn's friends and family, besides some of Rosea's Fairy friends, were drastically helped by the both of you."

Finn said, "I am guessing we are about to leave this time with you. I still have my promise to that farmer's son. I must enchant his crops and land beside his little friend's land. That is what he wished for, basically."

The Rolls was headed towards the grove. Rosea knew this and turned her attention back to what Lyreman was saying.

"The land is healthy. Finn, the locals all know that caring for the land is important. That's why you shook so much corn, and your friends even enchanted the land. Your promise was going on even when you were a child. The farmer is a young adult, and his life is still blessed by what you did that day. What we do now is mostly for the two of you." Lyreman said and then asked Finn to open his hand up. Then Lyreman placed a basic gold ring with a small red ruby in Finn's hand.

"What is that for?" Rosea asked.

Lyreman stated, "Don't lose this. I need to see this to know what you say is true when you get where you are going. Just call out my name when you arrive. Finn, you must tap the tip of your left shoe three times quickly after you say my name."

Finn placed the ring in his pocket with his coin. When they realized his coin was essential, Rosea had put extra stitching and fabric in that pocket. The car stopped, and Lyreman got out with them. It was dusk, and Lyreman spoke up,

"The two of you are like family. At this point, I am unsure if I ever see the two of you again. I have seen you in the past where both of you are headed. Just do me a favor and never tell someone anything about their future. You can help them, but don't tell them their fate. Bad things always happen and always will, and we will all eventually die. If you ever try to stop that. We can cause great harm to our own futures. I live with the knowledge of knowing how long a person will live. When I look at them, I see their final day. It is a heavy burden. The two of you live a long time. But don't be sad for those who do die. We enchanted do come back. Sometimes, it is just a new life in the enchanted world, or we are born to parents in the real world. Still, the knowledge of seeing people pass is a burden, especially when I have lived so long." Lyreman said with slight tears in his eyes.

Rosea hugged Lyreman; she realized he was dealing with the current knowledge that someone he knew would die soon. She only wished she could make that better.

Lyreman said, "Go into the grove, and when you see the Fairy lights, wish to go where you are needed. Imagine this area before trees grew here. Trust me. That will get you to where you need to be. Lyreman said this as the two started up the hill towards the grove."

Finn turned around at one point and saw Lyreman's head hung low. Something weighed on him more than their leaving. Lyreman was very sad. Finn turned back around before Lyreman noticed him looking.

Once inside the grove, Rosea and Finn stood under the trees. It was getting dark. The site had hundreds of orchids planted there, and many were in bloom. As the sun was almost gone, Fairy lights glided into the area and swirled around them and the flowers. Finn and Rosea moved to the grove's center, trying not to step on any plants.

"Hold my hand, Finn!" As he grabbed her hand, she started to wish to be where she was needed. She remembered that Lyreman stated It was before these trees were here. The light wind that always seemed to be moving through the grove stopped. Before them, a Fairy light circled a flower and touched one of its pedals. The flower lit up, and they could see the pinkish light the flower gave off started to engulf the whole area. Then they disappeared, and with this, the flower ceased to glow.

Chapter Thirteen

PROVINCIAL

FINN woke up on the ground with Rosea curled up next to him. The sun was just going down, and he stood to see where they were. The hill looked the same, but only a few small trees were there, with none of the grove trees present. Also, the nearby farm that grew corn where they came from no longer existed. The ground was just long green grass that had fallen over and was soft. Around the area were rocks and wildflowers like the time they had just come from. Finn helped Rosea up. He stood there wondering what was next. It took years to fix up that last cottage they lived in. He had no money besides the unique coin his family gave him and no idea how far back in time they had gone. As far as he knew, cavemen lived in the time they arrived!

"It looks the same, mostly," Rosea said as she stood there trying to hold back the excitement that she had just transported them! That meant she had her powers back. Well, at least she could travel to somewhere she realized she had chosen.

They both walked down to the nearby road. It had a couple of ruts in the dirt, left by very skinny tires, and a patch of tall grass was growing down the middle. The road didn't look used, and the once refined and well-cared-for gravel road was no longer present. Finn knew it was a few miles to town and figured he better do what Lyreman asked. Tapping his left shoe tip three times, he said, "Lyreman, Lyreman, We are here, Lyreman?"

From the distance, they could hear something coming down the road. It was a horse-drawn enclosed carriage. It was a very fancy one with a black polished lacquered finish and shiny polished lanterns hanging on the front of it. Two large black horses with long flowing manes and tails were pulling it. A small girl was sitting up high on a small seat, holding the reins. As it approached, the little girl said, "Whoaish, my boys!" and the horses stopped.

The little girl climbed down and went to the carriage door. Flipped down a small step below the door and then held the door open. Out of the carriage stepped Lyreman. He looked a lot younger but was still wearing very nice clothes. The clothes looked like something from a history book and looked expensive.

The little man said with a smile and a slight bow, "Hello, I am Lyreman. What has brought you to call on me tonight?"

Rosea and Finn tried to talk simultaneously, but Lyreman held up a hand and said, "Sorry, but only one at a time, please. First, the young man since he called my name. Repeatedly. You know, you only had to call me once? I am not human, and I definitely hear you call me. Also, you are supposed to tap your left toe tip three times after saying my name."

Finn spoke up, "Sorry about that, Lyreman. We are here because of you. You told us to come to this time and call your name."

Lyreman had a puzzled look on his face. He didn't remember these two. Well, not from this timeline. They were something new to him. Their spirits were old but much more recent than everything around them. They were from the future! He could see it all over them besides their clothing, which was very odd looking to Lyreman.

"Can you prove that I sent you here? I would have given you something to give me. I am that way." Lyreman said as he held out his hand.

Finn handed the small box he had been holding onto to Rosea. He reached into his pocket and got the ring out. He placed it into Lyreman's hand. At that point, Lyreman's face lit up with a smile.

Waving them into the carriage, he told the little girl, "Dawn, take us to my house. These two might be with us for a while." Lyreman then got inside, and they headed down the road.

The inside of the carriage was very plush. The walls and ceiling were all padded in soft, deep purple velvet. There were brass accents everywhere, and they all looked very polished. Finn looked at them wondering…

"Yes, my Dear boy. That is actually gold. I live very well, and that shouldn't surprise you since you are just like me. Now, I need to ask both of you your names. You seem to know mine, but I do not know the people you are. I have known many who have lived and returned over the years. Yet, somehow, I missed something with the two of you. So let's start with names and move from there." Lyreman said as he sat back and folded his hands in his lap.

Rosea said, "Well, I am Rosea, and this is my husband Finn. I am a Time Fairy, and Finn is a Leprechaun from the future. We can not tell you much since you warned us from telling people certain things. I can tell you that we won't ride in horse-drawn carriages that ride rough like this in the future. Horses are no longer used as work animals. You did send us here but did not say why."

Lyreman stated, "Well, this is the finest carriage ever made and has the best suspension, but obviously, the two of you are spoiled by the future. So I sent you? Well, I must figure this out. I agree with not sharing too much from the future. And even telling me that horses no longer pull carriages should not be said. Although that means I will be investing in whatever replaces them. Well, back to the issue at hand. I don't have much experience with Time Fairies, so please bear with me. I do have to ask. If horses don't pull carriages in the future, what animal does?"

Finn just started laughing as Lyreman looked on with a look of confusion.

"What is so funny?" Lyreman asked.

"You are an old man. You might be a lot younger now, but you are old! Very old from what you have told me in the future. You know so much but don't know anything but the past. You do not know the future. I know you can sense how long a person will live and their actual time of death. But you really can't see the future. It's funny almost." Finn said, realizing Rosea wasn't laughing with him.

"Ignore my husband. He forgets his manners at times. This time travel thing is new for me, and I sense the confusion can be great sometimes. Especially for those visited by people of the future." Rosea said, trying not to upset Lyreman. She knew they might be sleeping in a field come nighttime if he got angry.

"I get it. I really do. I understand nervous humor. And it is true I can sense when many will die and how. That isn't always the case. If I am too close to a person, I might not see it clearly for a friend or a loved one. I can care a lot for someone like a good friend and only see a glimpse of when they die and how. It's a gift and a curse. I blame the two of you for this curse!" Lyreman said.

Finn got greatly concerned. Lyreman was a force that no one ever could stop. He just accused them of a curse. This could not be good.

Lyreman said quickly and assuringly, "Don't worry, you two. It's not anything you did in this life. I know your spirits from back in time. You two are Niamh and Oisín. Which is your original names from the legends. I know the two of you. My dealings with you two allowed me to see a person's lifespan. The worst part is being around humans. They only live a short time compared to us. They come back in another body, but I see so many past lives when I look at them. It's so disturbing. Many make the same mistakes in life after life. No matter how many times they are reborn. They have different names and faces, but their spirit is always the same."

"You know us? But you acted as if you didn't know us in the future. Like it was the first time you met us. Why is that?" Rosea asked.

"Ha! You see. I must have known I could not tell you something. Meaning I needed to hide the truth from you. I would love to know how people travel without horses pulling them. I am sure that is magical. But we are arriving, and we can talk later." Lyreman said.

The carriage stopped in front of a lovely cottage. It had a nice thatched roof that Finn admired. It was the same house Lyreman lived in in the future. Finn had worked on its roof, which was always the best maintained around. Everyone exited the carriage, which then took off around the back and seemed to vanish. They went inside, and standing in the kitchen was Dawn! She was cooking something on the stove. She was there but had just driven off in the carriage.

Lyreman chuckled, "I see you are amazed at Dawn. Anyone who knows her realizes she is unique, considering she is still in a child's body. She just doesn't want to grow up. But I feel you might have met her from the looks on your faces. So, let's sit down and talk. First, I want the story on that little box you two have passed back and forth to each other."

Rosea placed the box on the table and opened it. Nothing was inside. Finn took out his lucky coin and put it inside, and Rosea closed the box.

Lyreman looked at them and asked, "What is that supposed to do?"

Rosea smiled and said. "I have no idea. You asked us to bring the box, and that's Finn's lucky family coin."

Lyreman said, "I will need more information from the two of you. I am a powerful Leprechaun, but I do not know what is happening here. I only know the two of you from a distant past life, and I am sure neither of you truly remembers. Maybe bits and pieces, but not everything. If you did, you would have run as soon as I stepped out of that carriage. You would have realized you wronged me. Again. I am way over that. Plus, my body has been reborn a few times since those days. I haven't died; I just become renewed. Those are old memories I just retained from my previous incarnations. So relax. I won't destroy you. At least at this point in time."

Lyreman chuckled and said, "Don't tell me about me or others from when you came. Tell me about this box. Where you got it and why that coin is important. I must figure out why I made you bring that box."

Finn and Rosea took turns telling Lyreman about the fairy orchid grove at the spot he picked them up from. They spoke about how they were stuck in their past about fifteen years from where they lived. Well, from where Finn lived. Rosea was originally from the time they got stuck in.

Lyreman just sat back and listened. He fired up his pipe and let them tell him everything. He snapped his fingers at one point, and the fireplace lit up. He listened very intently. He didn't seem surprised when they let slip out that a plane flew over the crops and dropped that fungicide. He didn't want to let them know he just learned about flying machines! He was highly interested in what they had to say and liked how Finn talked about improving the thatched roof business. Because he hated it when his roof leaked at times. Lyreman let them go on for a few hours. Dawn served them tea at one point and then dinner at another. Dawn disappeared at the end of the evening after stating she had to prepare the spare room.

At one point, Rosea told Lyreman about working at the Faerie Aislinn restaurant for Aislinn and Anders. She went on about learning how to use money and how Finn helped solve why the orchids were dying. The story about how she and Finn bought the microscope for Little Anders greatly interested Lyreman. The fact that Finn allowed the Farmer's son to catch him for wishes, not once but thrice, amazed him. Rosea also told him about the fairy slipper orchid glowing at the time they were transported to this current time where they were.

At this point, Lyreman stopped Rosea and asked, "The fairy light touched a flower when you transported?"

Finn said, "Yes. It glowed since we were under the canopy of the trees, and it was already dusk. It lit up the whole area in a pink shade."

"Well, congratulations to the both of you!" Lyreman said with a big smile.

Both Finn and Rosea said together, "What?"

"You are going to be parents. Seeing a Fairy light touch a flower at dusk is a sign. A Fairy light touching a flower any other time represents a Fairy being born. The fact you saw it at dusk means the two of you will have a child. The fact it happened at the time you were traveling is interesting. I am guessing you traveled with that baby." Lyreman said, looking at Rosea, who was rubbing her stomach, thinking about how hungry she had been the last few weeks.

Finn stood up, "I'm going to be a Dad! That is great. I can pass on the coin."

Lyreman said, "Have a seat, Finn. It is excellent news, but that coin and box are important. I believe they were a message to have you travel here. I think it's connected. I have an idea of how we should proceed. We all need sleep, and Dawn has prepared the two of you a room. She is very good at such things. It's the last room on the left. Just slide the used chamber pots under the flaps near the side wall. I will see the two of you in the morning."

"Splash!"

Finn woke up with water hitting his face. Rosea had dumped water from a pitcher on him, "Time to get up and get cleaned!" Rosea said as she snapped her fingers, and Finn found himself all cleaned and groomed. He noted that Rosea was even clean.

"How did you pull this off? I was worried since this place didn't have indoor plumbing, we would have only to bathe once a week or so since I have become accustomed to being clean due to you. Thank you so much!" Finn said.

Finn realized he would miss showers, but he would endure having water poured on him if he was clean. Plus, Rosea seemed to enjoy doing that to him. She took a sense of crude pleasure in dumping cold water on him.

They entered the kitchen, and Lyreman had some tomatoes, bread, and cheese cut up. They ate, and Lyreman took them outside. There, they noticed an old wagon being drawn by mules. Dawn was ready to drive them away.

Lyreman said, "I am sorry I can not help today. Dawn will take the two of you to where I picked you up. Bury that box with the coin in the middle of the area where the grass grows. Shovels, sapling starter trees, and water pitchers are in the back of the wagon. Please plant those trees where you remember them growing in the future. I also believe Dawn has packed a lunch for everyone. Whatever you do. Do not ask Dawn for help. She will just do her own thing. That spot is ancient and was the location of my first house in this area. It was meager and small, but it was all I needed back then. That's why the grass is so thick and green in that spot. We tore down that small cottage and built this one. We used stones and anything in good condition to make my new place. Dawn and I mostly used magic, but today, you need to plant those trees the old-fashioned way. You even need to water the area where you bury the wooden box. Place it in the center and at least six inches under the surface. Ensure the grass you removed is placed back on top and watered."

Lyreman just vanished. He really didn't need to be taken anywhere. He was a Leprechaun. He liked showing off his wealth and taking his time going places, so he owned a carriage. He hated rushing to get stuff done. He felt the world was always going faster and faster but losing the enjoyment of being alive.

Finn and Rosea dug holes all along the outer edge of the open grass area. Most of the trees they remembered had large and small rocks on the outside edge of them. So, they planted the trees far enough away to grow without hitting the rocks.

They thoroughly water the trees using pitchers to get water from the creek. Dawn only drove them there. She spent the whole day chasing butterflies and picking wild daisies. Dawn was acting how old she looked, which was the opposite of how old she was. Finn remembered Lyreman saying she was older than him, and he was hundreds of years old. She was older than even the legends of their previous lives. Which neither really remembered. Rosea had a few memories and knew she was once a legend but had once thought those memories were only from dreams. Finn was clueless. He didn't remember anything from any past life.

After all the trees were planted, they sat and ate. Dawn only stopped for a biscuit and some tea. Then she resumed chasing bugs and picking flowers. She ran around with a necklace from the assorted flowers she had chosen. After cleaning up, Finn grabbed the small box that Dawn had loaded in the wagon before they even woke up that morning. He grabbed a shovel and made a hole deep enough for the box. Placing it in the hole and pushing the dirt back over it. He put the dirt clump with grass on top, and Rosea watered it as Lyreman instructed.

Finn asked Rosea, "Did we plant enough trees? I remember many trees; we just had enough to encircle the green open area here."

"I wouldn't worry. These trees are a type of cedar that can live a very long time. Their seeds will make more trees in the next few hundred years. The birds, animals, and the wind will bring the rest of the seeds for other items. Having these trees grow here will start the ecosystem, encouraging many trees and shrubs to grow around this area. I believe Lyreman knows what he is doing. Plus, we never planted things in the past when we were born on enchanted lands. You just shook corn or whatever the farmers grew. You never had to plant things. Even though we buried seeds to watch stuff grow at times. We only ever grew reeds, thatch, and orchids. We can ask Lyreman later."

At that point, they heard. "SNAP!" Dawn had been running around and jumped off a nearby rock, and her foot landed on one of the tree saplings they just planted. Dawn stopped and lifted her foot. She had tears start down her face.

"I am sorry. I really am. Lyreman won't like me after this." Dawn said, standing there looking at the tree she had just killed.

Rosea came to Dawn and hugged her. Rosea knew from Future Dawn that no one ever touched her! And if you did, she went ballistic. But Rosea felt so sad for her that she hugged Dawn. With Finn watching in amazement, Dawn accepted the hug and even returned it.

"I wouldn't even worry about this tree." Finn stated while escorting the ladies down the path to the wagon, "I remember that we entered a larger gap between two of the trees in the future. It was exactly where you stepped on that tree. It wasn't supposed to be there. You did us a favor, Dawn. Thank you. We will tell Lyreman what a great help you were today. Without you, we might have done what Lyreman wanted us to do wrong. Thanks so much."

Dawn stopped crying and asked, "Really? I did good work? I like that." She stopped crying, entered the wagon, and drove everyone home.

Dawn was heard saying, "I do good work.", softly to herself on the way home.

Rosea looked at Finn and said, "You will make a great Dad. You handled that very well. Most men would overreact and then regret it later after the damage was done, and they couldn't undo the stuff they said. You just looked at the situation and handled it very well. Thanks. She must have a strange and hard life. We really did need her to do that today."

When they got to Lyreman's cottage, he let them know he was glad to see Dawn so happy. She was cleaning everything. Until then, Dawn cleaned, but this was a huge step up. It was the quality they saw in the future. They made what Dawn did more valuable. She really liked doing good work.

Lyreman stated, "Stepping on that extra tree is what Dawn always does. She has a strange luck of breaking or destroying things that would hurt us or negatively affect us. She is very unique."

Then Lyreman told them about how Dawn once lived at that old location where they planted the trees. "It was a small broken-down cottage, and Dawn lived there. She didn't know how to fix things and went there to sleep. I moved into the house temporarily and was watched as I fixed and cleaned things. When I was trying to set up this cottage, she also visited here. So we lived in that small shack until I got this new cottage we are in. I used lots of the stones from the other one and left the old wood and thatch to rot there. The large green area is where the house once was. Dawn still visits that site. That place is significant to her. It is also vital to many enchanted people in this area."

"Why is that?" Finn asked.

"Well, Dawn is ancient. She lived in the cottages in the area long before I arrived here. I inherited this job to watch the surrounding areas from my Dad. Whom I seldom ever see. When Dawn just followed me around, I adored her like a daughter. She eventually decided to live in this rebuilt cottage with me here. She told me she had lived on this land and around this cottage for a long time.

I didn't realize for years that the shack was on an actual portal between the enchanted and human worlds. It has some kind of power that is connected to Fairies being born. I am referring to both boys and girls. Leprechaun boys are different but still Fairies. This place mainly affects girl Fairies. So Dawn was drawn to it. She has no family that any of us know of. If she had anybody that was a distant relative, she would be drawn to them. It never happens. We think she is stuck in the enchanted life forever. She never ages and goes from being mentally mature to childlike at random.

I hope to find something that one day helps her become stable in either form. It is hard to constantly adjust to her moods as she goes from one person to the next. Dawn always wanted me to rebuild that old shack so she could stay there, but the trees would be a better option. Because it will create a type of home for Fairies living in the dream world. And I am excited to see who eventually cultivates those orchids."

Lyreman let Finn and Rosea stay with him. He stated that they would eventually return to their original time. Still, for now, they were helping balance the enchanted world. They could even help undo the damage their own choices in the past had created. And although they had wronged him many years ago, he knew it wasn't him they had to make amends to. They had to balance things. Finn did well with the negative energy released on the Farmer's land in the future. He was amazed at how brave Finn was, but he knew Finn was paying a debt to the enchanted world because balance was being sought. Lyreman realized who they were now was impacting his life and others for good. He was still figuring it out but longed to talk to his future self. It would save a lot of time and guesswork.

Chapter Fourteen

SAME PERSON

GROWING as time went by, the trees at the grove flourished. Finn and Dawn would drive out and water them to ensure the roots grew deep enough to survive. Rosea decided to stay at home most days, along with Finn and her baby girl. They could not believe how happy they were.

This little girl had the same eyes as Aislinn, who owned the Faerie Aislinn restaurant. Rosea and Finn knew this was the same Aislinn. So they called her that. Dawn had a friend to play with, and even Lyreman tried to show he didn't care, but he always showed up with biscuits from the market for Aislinn. One day, as everyone was hanging out getting warm by the fireplace on a cold winter night, Lyreman came in.

Lyreman joined them to get warm and said, "She is as beautiful as she was when the two of you had her lifetimes ago when we were all friends."

Finn looked at Lyreman and asked, "How so?"

"Well," Lyreman continued, "Aislinn is your daughter. She will always be your daughter. The two of you never time travel much, and what little I know about Time Fairies is only from the two of you."

Lyreman approached the fire and rubbed his hands to spread the fire's warmth on them.

Lyreman continued, "Aislinn will always be born to the two of you. You will bump into her at different parts of her life but may not even know it's her. I have usually been there to foster your relationship with her. Aislinn always leaves when she is five, like most enchanted children do. She always goes to the dream state and returns when she meets the correct man. Usually, she isn't gone long. I know from what you have told me. You will not see her for hundreds of years after she leaves. You already knew her when she was older than both of you. That in itself is a miracle. I am glad I will be part of that. But, unfortunately, when you both return to Finn's correct time. Aislinn will already be gone again."

"Gone? You mean?" Rosea asked in a panic.

Lyreman looked at them and said, "Yes. She will cease to be alive. I have looked at her life force, which ends long before you. It seems very short. It hurts me to say this, even if she was a human, but you two must know this. I have known Aislinn before. She never had a short lifespan except once. She usually lived a very long time. The problem with telling you this is what I told you in the past during her short life. The both of you tried to save her, and many enchanted died. We can't ever save a person if we know they will die. We can not bring them back or make their life longer. We are not allowed to change death. It isn't something we control."

"We can do anything! Do we have to let her die?" Finn said, slightly angry.

"Yes," Lyreman stated and continued. "You tried last time and destroyed everything. Aislinn still died soon after you saved her, but so did many enchanted along with humans whose lives were changed because you delayed her death."

Aislinn was playing near the fire. She was about three and unaware of the conversation they were having. Dawn left the room. She wanted to avoid hearing about Aislinn going. Everyone left her eventually. Dawn was the only one who stayed. She knew that Lyreman would leave at some point, even though she was unsure when or how he would eventually leave her.

"Both of you have some soul-searching to do. You got to be friends with Aislinn for a few years. You both should be happy with that. Most enchanted parents just forget them when they go to the enchanted realm and never see them again or remember them. You are different. You get to remember some stuff, although Finn is more forgetful.

Well... He's much more forgetful since you married him in your first life, and the two of you became famous legends. Something neither of you truly remembers. Real shame. You two were glorious like God's almost. Rosea was known for her beauty, and Finn was a military hero. Finn wasn't allowed to visit his family once married except once every fifteen years. Does fifteen years seem familiar to you?" Lyreman said, looking at them, knowing they did not like what he said.

"No!" Finn said, "I do not believe I am subject to some fifteen-year curse in every life. That just wouldn't be right. What did I ever do to deserve this?"

Lyreman just laughed and patted Finn on the back, "Nothing. You did nothing. That Fifteen-year thing is a holdover from what Rosea's Dad did in the past. It keeps showing up. Usually, it's a fifteen-year thing. I would bet you don't see your parents and friends for that length of time from the last time they saw you. Don't stress. You may be only missing fifteen years. Your family may not even notice you are gone. Plus you could see them sooner. Fifteen years is the amount of time that shows up, and you might have already done that by initially going back in time for fifteen years, as you have told me. It is not always the length you are separated."

Finn and Rosea were accepting what Lyreman told them. They realized they just needed to enjoy their time with

Aislinn and be grateful she was in their lives as an adult, even if out of time. It was another thing Lyreman had given them.

It was as if Lyreman went out of his way to tell them something he wasn't supposed to. So the two just enjoyed their time with Aislinn. The trees they planted were only a few feet tall. But they often took Aislinn to the spot to play on the soft green grass. She and Dawn tried to catch butterflies and made flower necklaces. Well, Dawn made the necklaces, and Aislinn wore them. The next few years flew by. Everyone did their best to do everything they could with Aislinn. They knew she would leave as soon as it was time. She had always left in the past, according to what Lyreman said. They knew this was true since even Lyreman spent time with Aislinn as if she were his granddaughter, and time was running out.

That fateful day came and went very fast.

On Aislinn's fifth birthday, everyone gathered at the trees and celebrated where Aislinn was spinning her dress after watching Dawn do the same thing. Then, without warning, Aislinn just vanished as a little green Fairy light and wisped away. Not one person had dry eyes when that happened. Although they knew it would happen at any moment. Lyreman, who never touched anyone, Hugged Finn, Rosea, and even Dawn. He tried to hide his tears. Then, knowing it was necessary, Lyreman choked back his tears and reached into his pocket. He removed that ring that Finn had put into his hand years earlier. He asked Finn to put out his hand.

Then Lyreman placed the ring into Finn's hand and said,

"When you meet me in the future, please return this to me. I must get this back. I still have my original ring, which I will carry forward and give you. You need to give this back, so I have it again. Because it is time we are trying to appease."

Rosea was still tearing up very hard, "Now? Must we do this now? I just lost my daughter, and you are asking me to do this now?"

Lyreman never got used to this. He had seen many vanish countless times, and it always was tough. He knew Rosea would eventually forget that Aislinn was her daughter. But would always remember her friend Aislinn in the future or the Aislinn who owned the orchid grove. She would remember that Aislinn and even being told that the adult version was her daughter. But she would never remember the child version that just disappeared. He knew this would pass, but the pain was real, and he wished it didn't have to be because he could never forget. He remembered every time a child left and had watched many parents fall apart. He knew Rosea and Finn would hold onto Aislinn's memory as long as possible. But unfortunately, they would sooner or later lose to what the enchanted rules declared.

"Yes, Rosea and Finn. Now is the time both of you must move on. It is back to your true time, Finn. I believe you will be able to visit me throughout the years. I sure hope so. I will see you in the future, but please don't make me wait long. Rosea just held Finn's hand, and as tears streamed down her face, she thought of home. Remember the last time both of you were there. Don't worry. I am sure both of you will be fine. It isn't sad she is gone. She is becoming what we all must become. It's just painful to be without them for a short time. We always see them again. Most just don't realize that." As Lyreman said this, Finn and Rosea vanished with a swirl of pink sparkles and light green Fairy lights.

"Now what?" Dawn asked Lyreman with tears in her eyes.

"Don't worry, Dawn. You will forget about this by tomorrow. And you will, as usual, do an outstanding job at cleaning the cottage like you always do. It is now time we find someone else who needs our help. On the other hand, I will keep trying to figure out why you have no relatives from the past to whom you are drawn. We will figure this out. Next, we need to find out who to sell that grove of trees to. I feel we need to get that into the hands of whoever Aislinn marries when she finds the right man. Seems to me that won't be for a few hundred years. Lucky us, we might see her every so often when she decided to become human like we did in the past. She always comes back and marries the same spirit in a man each time. His name changes also, but it's usually the same guy. Only Aislinn's name is always the same. One day, I'll figure out why. Let's go, Dawn. You helped me do good work again." As Lyreman said this, they headed down the path to the carriage.

Chapter Fifteen

THE TRIP

ZIPPING through time, Finn and Rosea had never heard noises in the past. Those trips happened fast, and usually, they were unaware they were transported to another time. But this trip made them feel like they were traveling for hours. There was a slight howling noise, and they felt content. What neither one of them realized was they had forgotten about Aislinn. They were in an enchanted tunnel that led back to their time. Since the laws were more substantial here, they were being held so they would not be in pain anymore. The rules were not meant to be mean. Without those rules, all enchanted life would die out. It was about matching people with those they were meant to be with, and sometimes, that took many years of waiting.

With an explosion of light, the two stood again before the fire at Finn's parent's house. The friends and family were still there from the night they disappeared. Everyone started to clap.

"Congratulations, Finn and Rosea! I am so glad that the two of you are back.", Finn's Mom stated.

Finn's Dad turned to his wife and asked, "What do you mean they are back?"

Rosea said, "I am delighted all of you are here tonight. What might not surprise any of you since we are all enchanted folk but will amaze you is Finn and I have been together for many years. That all happened in the last few seconds. It will also explain why we are in these silly provincial clothes right now."

Finn's father said, "What we saw looked like you transformed your marriage garments into travel clothes. Tell us more!"

"Well. We went back fifteen years and couldn't visit you because the younger me was here. We lived in a cottage down the road." Finn paused, but then Rosea took over, "Finn is being modest. He is why the old Farmer left, and the son took over the farm here. Finn would be reluctant to tell anyone that he actually is the person who removed the curse from these lands years ago. I am sure there is much more we can say to you, but we just got married years ago and are very tired now. Can we just stay here tonight, Mom?" Rosea said, looking at Finn's Mom.

"Of course, Daughter, Anything you want. Thanks for bringing my son back." Finn's Mom said as she told everyone they would get together in a few days to share information.

As Finn and Rosea got ready for bed, they snuggled into that wool fluff that was in Finn's room. They enjoyed being small again and forgetting the human world for a minute. They were both drained and just wanted to sleep. And both felt as if they had been through a lot.

Finn told Rosea as they drifted off to sleep, "It is so nice to be home. I just feel as if we are missing something. It's probably just my coin I left in that box we buried. But I feel like I lost something."

The following day, Finn and Rosea came downstairs to see Lyreman sitting down and talking to Finn's parents. Finn's Mom hugged Rosea, saying, "I am so sorry to hear this. It is a shock, but at least we know that great lady was your Daughter."

"Daughter? What Daughter?, Rosea said.

Finn put his hand on Rosea's shoulder and tilted his head in anguish, saying, "That's what I lost,... what we lost. I felt this loss I could not explain. Why? I wanted to remember having a child."

Finn's Dad stood up and said, "Son, it seems cruel, but we should take a trip with Lyreman today. It would help from what he just told me."

Outside, the Rolls sat waiting, and everyone became human-sized and got into it. The car headed down the road. No one spoke. It was a sad situation for everyone. The Rolls turned down some back roads towards a small church. Behind it was a small cemetery where The Butler drove to. Everyone got out and followed Lyreman. He walked a ways and stopped at the most prominent gravestone with a large carved and intricate cross above it. The gravestone read, "Aislinn, a great friend to all." No one questioned the stone; it had no last name. The Enchanted practiced never saying last names. If a person had their full name, they could control them. Even in death, they left off the last name. The general public never realized it. If they did, they disregarded it and thought nothing more about it.

Lyreman said, "I know this is unfortunate for everyone, especially the both of you. Finn and Rosea, you just got married in everyone's eyes around here, but you have been through a lot. Since I was there in the past, I can say what great parents you were and why Aislinn's favorite place existed. You planted the trees in the past and even saved the orchids that ended up here years later by her husband's family. Part of my job was watching over her for years as a Fairy spirit and in human form. She was one of my best friends. I already knew when I sent both of you back in time Aislinn and her husband only had days to live, and nothing could save them. Their life energy was up. Another car crashed into them, and they didn't realize the other car didn't heed the stop sign. Aislinn was a great lady; she is what all enchanted try to be. She was delighted to know the two of you when you lived here in the past. I told all of you she was your child then. It is rare for me to know and be able to share this info with anyone. Aislinn is unique. We will see her again. I know that."

Lyreman had a tear fall from his eyes. Everyone else there was crying. Although Finn and Rosea cried for Lady Aislinn, they had no memory of their Daughter as a child. They cried because they could not remember that. Their journey did not seem to give them rest. They felt tired again from this heavy burden. Finn and Rosea headed to the car and waited for everyone else to join them. Everyone talked about how they should try and find things the two could do that would help them adjust to life again. They just came from a few hundred years ago, and a start would be replacing the clothes they wore. They were dressed almost clown-like in the modern era and stood out, which was never suitable for the enchanted. They all eventually got into the car, and they drove off.

"Please drive us to the cottage," Lyreman asked.

"Yes, sir. We will be there shortly.", The Butler stated.

No one noticed, but The Butler also had tears in his eyes. He knew what losing a family member and close friend was like. And Aislinn was a close friend of his. Since his own Daughter wouldn't talk to him. Aislinn even included him in family outings. Sometimes, he felt like her father, and she even asked him for advice, which he missed most from his own Daughter.

The car pulled up to Finn and Rosea's cottage. Finn looked at Lyreman and asked, "It's still here? Do we still own it after all this time?"

"It's all yours. It always has been my friend. Coilin and Faolan helped me take care of this place. If they did, I offered to buy them a few farm supplies over the years. I think they would have helped for free. Plus, Dawn said she missed both of you. She kept the inside perfect and let us know if anything needed attention that she couldn't fix. Now the roof needs work. It never leaked, but the thatch is very thin and needs repair." Lyreman said as he felt the loss these two were feeling. He knew and couldn't help but feel their pain. And although many humans desired to be magical and be enchanted. Still, none of them had any idea what many magical people had to endure daily.

Finn reached into his pocket as everyone started to leave the two at the cottage. He handed Lyreman the ring, saying, "Thanks for everything. I know you have always tried to make our lives as nice as possible. I just hope I can return the favor one day."

Lyreman hugged Finn, "Finn, you don't owe me anything. Your Daughter was a blessing to everyone, and she always is in every life. We will see her again because this is just a new beginning. Plus, you have always given back. You and Rosea have done more for everyone in this area than you will ever know. There is actually good news in this for you and Rosea. So don't worry. I am working on something and will see the two of you in a few days. So please just relax and get your bearings. And do not time travel! I mean that! There is stuff here you will want to be a part of. Oh... I almost forgot. You both are now in control of your magical powers again. So don't go crazy with it."

The following week went by fast. Dawn was always there making food and hanging out. She missed them a lot. They never realized till now, but she acted that way when she first worked for them. She must have missed them from when she first met them hundreds of years ago. She had never changed. Dawn was still a busy body cleaning and fixing all she could except the roof and a few walls. The house needed a fresh coat of paint. She didn't paint anything outside. It looked old and rundown, and weeds had taken over the yard. She was a great house Fairy but had no idea how to be a yard Fairy.

Rosea got straight to work getting the yard in order. Finn couldn't figure out what his friends did to help keep the farm running. He didn't see the house outside looking good, and the yard was a wreck! Finn hoped Lyreman didn't pay those guys a lot. Then he saw that the fields were still being managed and crops grown. What did they do with the produce? They still didn't do roofs, did they? Those two did other stuff now. Well. He figured he would see what was going on in the thatch shop. When Finn opened that shop, he saw stacks of reeds and thatch dried, cut, and sorted into piles. It was more than enough for him to redo his roof.

What stood out the most was his panel van. It was still there, cleaned and polished, and did not look fifteen years older. The tires were new, and the inside was immaculate. However, the little red car sitting outside all those years had faded and rusted, besides accumulating more dents from teenagers learning to drive. It was already old, but now it would need a lot more bodywork, and magically, the seat was still brand new, probably from an enchantment from Lyreman. Outside, he heard a vehicle drive up. It was his two friends, Coilin and Faolan.

"Long time no see, friend," Coilin said to Finn.

"It sure has been. What have you two been doing, and how does my truck look new?" Finn asked.

Faolan said, "Well, friend, we needed to keep that old bucket up and running these last few years. You have been gone a long while. We both kept up the repair of the roofs you used your plastic invention on. They needed a little work every so often. We didn't create new accounts since we also had lots to do on our farms."

"You two didn't have to do that. That was very kind of you." Finn stated.

Coilin said with a smile, "You know Faolan, He isn't always straightforward except how he doesn't believe in magical people. Let me tell you straight. Lyreman said he would buy us farm equipment if we kept your farm and business running. So we did what we could over the years when we did basic roof mend and grew crops that other thatchers used. We made profits. That money is what Lyreman let us use to buy farm equipment. We also acquired some land in a few areas.

So Faolan isn't being straight with you. We needed the money and the blessings your farm and business gave us. Your fields still produce the best reeds and thatch. We made a lot of money. That's where you make out well. Lyreman stated that we were to give all the extra profit to Dawn for her to put in the bank. I am unsure how a child can do banking, but Lyreman said to do it. And we don't question him."

"Thanks, guys. I really appreciate it. No matter the motive. You kept my farm going. It will take me a while to repair my own house, but the bones of my business are still going strong. Thanks. Now that I am here. Let me know if you need help." Finn said earnestly.

Faolan said. "Sorry, we can't stay long. We are headed to Tiffany's tunnels. She added a few more to grow cherry trees in! We are going to see if she needs help. My sister can be needy at times." Faolan had a big smile, knowing his sister needed his help–something he took pride in.

The guys drove off, and Finn went inside to ask Dawn, "We have money? How much?"

Dawn walked him over to a spare closet and opened a door. There was money stacked to the ceiling. She then took him to an extra room where money was piled high in one corner. Then she pointed to under the bed. Finn got on his hands and knees and saw that money was stacked tight under the bed, and it was all in large bills. He even saw a trash can in the room full of gold coins.

"That is a lot of money Dawn. It is hard to believe the guys made that much extra money after using some to buy farm equipment. How did we get so much?"

Dawn giggled, "I used some and invested in local stocks because Lyreman said I needed to learn to make money in case he was not around. He said he worried I might struggle without him, but after that, I made a little more and so much. Then he said he was no longer worried. I actually don't use money. What because what little Lyreman gave me, I could buy stuff to fix this house and see it clean. Plus, I have my own ways to get things. This house needs work, but I would have never let it fall apart. I also have more money in stocks I haven't sold yet. Do you want that also?" Dawn asked.

"Oh No, Dawn. You can keep the money in those stocks. You can do whatever you wish with it. Consider it your reward for running stuff while I was gone.", Finn said.

"It is almost as much as I have stashed under that bed. Are you sure? It is more money than most make in their lives.", Dawn said, looking concerned.

"Dawn, you are a unique person. You can keep that money since you have actually earned it. You deserve it for doing such a good job. It will be the money Lyreman was worried you would need someday. You have it now. If you have too much, I advise you to donate some to those in need or use it to give really cool Saint Nicholas gifts to the less fortunate in the area. You seem to be very good at making money. I am sure you will make more. Just give some away every time you double what you have. Buy Lyreman a gift. That is something he won't ever see coming." Finn was impressed by Dawn and hoped he relayed that to her.

Rosea walked into the room Dawn and Finn was in, "You are joking, right? Is that ours? What will we use all that for?"

Dawn walked out to go clean something again, probably.

Finn raised his eyebrows and said. "Yes, it is also ours. If you're struggling with this huge stack of money, don't look under the bed or in the spare closet. I told Dawn to keep the rest she had in stocks as payment for making our money grow. You can get a new pickup truck or whatever you want because I saw the car, and it has rusted apart, sitting for so many years. Bringing the panel truck in and getting it tuned up and fluid changes should be all it needs for me. It's a nice-looking truck that looks surprisingly better than when we left. Since we can do whatever you want. I say we fix this place and figure out the cash thing later. It would be best if we started to deposit all of this into a bank. Except for those gold coins. I think I will keep those in our house."

Rosea was still processing Aislinn and all their adventures in the past, but she would have liked all of this money with a family. She once had plans to improve their life, but now, it was just money. She knew that she would feel different one day, but at the moment, nothing could undo her sense of loss. Finn looked at her, knowing she would take time to overcome this. He wanted to figure something out. He knew she needed a project. Something she could keep busy with until she came to terms with things. Finn wasn't OK, but he figured she would require him to remain strong now. They always wanted a child. And forgetting her seemed so cruel.

Chapter Sixteen

PANTRY SUPPLIES

UNKNOWINGLY, a month had passed, and Finn and Rosea had started to get the cottage looking better. On this day, Finn struggled to mow the grass in the yard and could only cut some of it. He had no magic skills to trim it, and the borrowed mower was not designed to cut weeds a few feet tall. So he only did part of the yard, and that was after much effort. The short stubble instantly turned into bright green grass, which was how it always looked when they lived there. Finn looked at it in amazement, wondering how weeds grew in an area still holding so much magic. After giving up, he went inside to get a drink of water.

"Knock, Knock, Knock..." sounded from the front door. Finn and Rosea went to see who it was.

Opening the door, there was Finn's Mom standing there, "Hello, Son and Daughter. I am here to ask a favor. I know a lot has gone on, but I have waited a long time for Finn to return to his current time. We really need your help."

"Come in, Come in," Rosea said to her.

Finn got his Mom a hot cup of tea, helped her to the recliner, and continued drinking his glass of water.

"Mom. What's so important that you had to wait almost fifteen years? And you have also waited over a month to come here after we showed back up. Why are you coming here in secret and human-sized?" Finn asked, overly concerned.

"First, I wanted you to settle in a bit before burdening you with this. And well, It is that cat. It is so smart that we can't get supplies from the Farmer's pantry. We are being forced to do without. It almost got your Dad the other day." Finn's Mom stated as she seemed rattled and said, "That Farmer's son has never harmed us. He seems to come after us but has never harmed anyone. We are not sure he is trying to catch us, but we are unwilling to find out."

Rosea assured her, "We have enough to give you whatever you want. Supplies are very cheap for The Enchanted when you are still small."

Rosea brought over some biscuits and a crumble cake for Finn's Mom. She was human-sized and probably very hungry because of that. It was a good decision since the biscuits and cake disappeared as Finn's Mom ate quickly.

"I am sorry for eating like this. I am nervous and haven't been human size but a few times. I forgot how hungry one can be like this." Finn's Mom said as she finished off a biscuit.

Finn tried to keep a straight face. He remembered how hungry he was the first time he was human-sized. So, he held back his laughter as he said, "Mom, I can supply whatever you need, but I do know we are at a very far distance, and you only need so little every so often. I have another plan if you give me a day or so.

"Well, That is great. I will leave now. I do not wish to be so big and hungry any longer. Before I leave, can I bother you for a small amount of Sugar, Honey, Flour, and Butter?" Finn's Mom stated as she stood up.

"That is no problem at all," Rosea said as she placed the items in tiny plastic sealable bags from when she collected Orchid seeds. And these were very little bags. Rosea made minor cuts in the tops of the bags for handholds.

Finn's Mom shrunk down, grabbed the handholds in the tops of the tiny bags, then said her goodbyes as she walked towards the door and vanished.

"OK, Mister! What kind of crazy idea do you have? I know you. It must be a crazy idea." Rosea said, looking sternly at Finn.

They headed to the Farmer's house in the panel truck the next day. Finn knocked on the door of the Farmer's house. Rosea didn't wish to go inside. She stayed in the truck. The Farmer answered the door and invited Finn inside after Finn said he would like to talk for a few minutes and assured the Farmer it would be worth his time.

The Farmer's wife brought in tea and excused herself to prepare dinner. She was the little girl that was friends with the Farmer's son. She was a lot older now and still just as pleasant.

"What is so important, Finn? I remember you from when I went to Little Anders's birthday party. You don't seem like you have aged much. I think I know why. So why don't we step outside where no one else can hear?" The Farmer said as they stepped into the yard and walked around the tractors and implements.

The Farmer's son said, "I must act as if we are talking about tractors. My wife does not know about my deal and wishes with you."

"What?... How do you know?" Finn asked.

The Farmer smiled, "I didn't, but I had a hunch. You just admitted to it. I realized as a little boy that your face was hard to focus on. I realized I could see your face clearly in a small water puddle near us. It wasn't perfect since the wind kind of made ripples in it. But I remember that face. I always thought you looked like that Leprechaun."

"You are a tricky one. I guess there is no fooling you? So I will tell you what I am dealing with." Finn said.

"Well, let me break the ice, Finn. I have known your name since that birthday party, but I will not use it against you. Plus, I do not know your last name. So that makes you safe. You have known my name, Danny, for many years. I am sure all of your people heard my Dad yell my name when I was younger. With that, I will offer my apologies again for what he did. So let's hear what you need from me. You have helped me a lot and those I know. Listening is the least I can do." Danny said with a smile on his face.

"Now that's how I thought this would go." Finn stated as he went on, "I have a favor to ask. I am willing to pay you whatever you feel is reasonable. My family, who still live near the area, need supplies. They are those who were always going into your pantry. It was never rodents of any sort. Rodents stay away from us. We are not really sure why, but rodents do not like us. Wherever we go, they stay away from that area. So you never needed that cat." Finn was saying.

"So what is the question? I feel the cat is the issue." Danny stated.

"That's it. That's the issue exactly. A cat is one of the few animals that do not respect us. They see us as food. My family and friends have visited that farmhouse for many years. They don't take much. They don't eat much but can't get some items without great effort. Like I said, I will pay you to supply items to them. Money isn't an issue. We never considered it theft since being on your land enchants it, which is why it does well. Except for that unfortunate past situation that you and I had to fix." Finn said, knowing he was risking lots with his disclosure, but felt Danny was very trustworthy.

"Finn, I admire you. I have read many books about your kind and kept your secret for years. Not even my wife knows about you. She knows I believe in Little People and tries not to give me grief since my father died claiming Little People had taken over his land. So it's a tricky deal for me. My children are intrigued by Leprechaun stories, and I am hoping to instill good views about your people in them. This is hard since I can not tell them about you. I know what you did to help me and my farm, and that Lyreman fellow was not my Uncle! He did help me and find a real relative to raise me until I was of age." Danny said as he walked to another piece of tractor equipment, pointing as if he was conversing about that item.

Finn walked over, pretending to look at what Danny pointed to as he said, "This is why I am here, Danny. I think we can solve both of our situations and become better off. I am willing to make another deal, but first, tell me why you chase my kind in the fields. I hear you don't want to harm anyone, but you seem to chase them."

Danny's eyes lit up. He had dreamed about meeting this Leprechaun again, and here he was. So Danny said, "Finn, I wasn't trying to catch anyone. I could never get close enough to ask them anything before they ran too fast or vanished. I wanted to talk to you again. I wanted to tell my wife about you because I dislike hiding things from her. She doesn't deserve any deception from the person she trusts the most in this world. It is tough for me to withhold the truth from her."

Finn agreed with him by nodding. Then, he offered a solution, "I have a way we can both get what we need, but that will require wishes and a deal. So I will go home and think of three wishes, and I want you to do the same. Visit me at my cottage in a few days. I think we can work out something."

"I want to do that, but you brought your wife. I think you should come inside and have dinner with us. My wife has a large meal she was making tonight. It usually lasts a few days, but she would love dinner guests. She never gets out much after our children were born. You would be doing me a favor. Please." Danny said.

Finn accepted, and Danny went to tell his wife. Finn asked Rosea to come into the house for dinner. She was very reluctant. Rosea was worried they might be in danger since Finn gave this Farmer wishes.

The Dinner went well. Rosea and Danny's wife, Heather, got along as if they were long-lost friends. Rosea could tell that Heather didn't seem magical, but she thought she knew her from the fairy dream world but could not remember anything. The children had come down for dinner and were very nice and friendly, like their parents. Finn could see in Rosea's eyes that she wished she had children like these. He knew that was impossible. They would permanently lose theirs and forget them. He knew that never stopped enchanted people from having children. He knew that only in some situations the children never had to leave. Finn pushed these thoughts aside and continued to enjoy the evening. Heather even sent them home with leftovers and a jar of her strawberry preserve.

A few days went by. Danny stopped by and found Finn in the field near the cottage harvesting thatch.

"That seems like the hard way? Can't you just snap your fingers or something?" Danny said as he approached Finn.

"You have jokes. I wish it were always that easy. Not all of us can do the same kind of things. I so wish I could do that kind of stuff. Me and my wife lack basic enchanted magic to use in daily life. I can only make wishes and deals besides enchanting the soil." Finn said with a look of consideration.

"Well, that changes my wishes a little, but I think I have come up with some wishes and a deal we can both live with. Why don't you take a break and take a trip with me." Danny said as Finn put down his thatch sickle. Finn was tired anyway. Cutting reeds was backbreaking work.

Danny had Finn hop into his truck and headed back towards his farmland. Danny took a dirt road. It was a road Finn knew all too well. It was the one that went right by the trees where his family and friends lived. Danny pulled over and parked where Lyreman always parked the Rolls.

They got out, and Danny just looked at him and said, "I have always known where they lived and have respected that since I was a little boy. I didn't come here because I was afraid they would leave. Knowing they help my crops, I left them alone unless I saw them in the crops. I just tried to talk to them, which never panned out. So, I suggest you get as many out here to hear my wishes as possible. It will help them to hear our deal. I will stand at a distance until you get some out here."

Finn talked to many for a few hours. He went tree to tree and even the holes in the ground where others lived. They just wouldn't come out. Then Finn's Mom walked out with his Dad, and they stepped towards Danny. They called everyone to come out and stated that this Farmer was the one who made the wishes as a boy who healed the land after it was cursed. They insisted everyone come out. Slowly, a few showed up on the outskirts. Then, a few more showed up. They wouldn't go near Danny, but that didn't matter.

"OK, Danny, Please tell them the deal and the wishes we discussed on the way here," Finn said, looking at all the Little People. Finn was also small at this point. He stepped to the side of Danny to show his trust in him.

Danny knelt to address everyone, "First, I will apologize for what happened all those years ago. I had no control over that event, and it saddened me too. I am grateful for what Finn and Lyreman have done for me. This is why I will do this for you today. Here is my gratitude.

First, I have agreed to get rid of my cat. It will leave the house in a few days. I promise never to get another one. Any animal I am thinking about getting in the future, I will pass by you before I get it. Just in case they are a danger to you. My Aunt loved that cat when she visited; my children want her to have it. So, it was easy to keep this agreement.

Second, I will make sure that supplies will be left out for all of you to get without needing to come into my house and struggle to get into the pantry. We will talk about that later in detail. I ask that you keep enchanting my crops and stay on my land. You do not need to pay me for the supplies. You have done more for me than I can ever repay you.

Third, My wishes that Finn will allow me to have will not be for me. I can not wish for more wishes, but I can wish for you to have wishes. It is a twist on what Finn wanted, but this is better. I have saved up lots of money from excellent crop harvests. All of my equipment is paid for, and I have more than enough to send my children to better schools if that is what they want when they grow up.

Fourth, It isn't required, but I hope some of you will move into my barn and tractor sheds. I am also okay with some of you setting up under the house. Let me know if I need to build anything that gives you a secure place. Just you being there will help keep the rodents away. Plus, it would be an excellent shelter for our heavy storms. Finn told me those were rough at times. The house is off the ground, and I have meant to put a brick skirt around the bottom to keep large animals out. Now, I will do it to create a place for you to shelter."

As Danny finished, he was amazed to see so many Little People come out and get closer to him. Many wore clothes, but some wore stuff made from tree bark, woven grasses, and fur. They all were amazed that a human wasn't trying to grab them. It was very unusual. Danny could not believe he wished for this since he was a boy. He wanted to be part of their world, and there they were, waiting for him to make wishes.

Finn asked everyone, "Do you have any questions before Danny starts wishing? I do want to remind you that Danny isn't the normal human we run from. So do not ever do this unless you know it's safe. Most times it isn't."

Finn stepped in front of Danny and stuck his foot out. Danny gently reached down, lightly pinched Finn's shoe, and said, "I've got you!"

Then Danny started with his wishes,

"For the first wish, I would like for every enchanted person on my land to be able to have one wish. They can ask for whatever they want. I hope this works out for everyone.

For my second wish, I ask for everyone living in Finn and Rosea's cottage to have all the enchanted powers they desire.

My final wish is personal but will safeguard everyone. I wish my family could know about you without it being dangerous for any of us. This is an odd wish and might not work, but I had to try."

"It is done!" Finn said this as he vanished and reappeared near his parents.

The Enchanted didn't know how to respond and had never seen a human do anything positive for them. They still didn't want to get too close to Danny but had a new respect for him. His wishes proved to them he was worth trusting. However, they were still waiting to test that trust.

Chapter Seventeen

TOO MUCH POWER

DANNY drove Finn home. He couldn't help but realize that Finn had a smile more extensive than he had ever seen on anyone. Looking over at Finn, he asked, "Why such a smile? I am happy also, but what gives?"

"I can have any enchanted power I want! You have no idea what that means to me and my wife. We can visit our Daughter in the fairy realm. We can use powers we never thought were possible. You have set us free.

Most importantly. Our Daughter who died can be visited. We can find a form of peace. She might not know us, but that will be okay," Finn said with slight tears in his eyes.

"Well, Finn, "I actually get it. When my wishes were granted, I was given knowledge of you and your people. I understand what it means to you. I also understand why my wife and Rosea got along so well. Until that wish, I only knew my wife was adopted. I never knew she was the child of a Fairy. She was raised by her adoptive Mom, who always amazed me with how she raised such an incredible person. I was given a lot more than I thought I asked for. The understanding I have has brought me great happiness and sadness. It's equal, so I can show how I feel. My children are safe because they are here past the age of five. Just a little enchanted. I wonder if my wish made this all come true or if it revealed this to me.

It doesn't matter. I don't understand how a Fairy could give up a child since I understand that Fairies do not wish to do this on purpose. I know that when I became friends with Heather as a young boy. It changed my life for the better. She was the positive influence I needed. That one wish was so powerful. When I wished I had powers as a child, it was a simple looking-at-a-shooting-star kind of wish. And lacked the real magic that a Leprechaun like you has. I now feel better knowing I can protect those on my land who chose to live the original way they have for centuries." Danny said.

Finn was dropped off at his cottage. Danny couldn't wait to talk to his wife about all of this. Before he drove off, Finn had him roll the window down and was told, "Oh. You do have powers. I was given the power to have any enchanted ability I wanted. That means I can do anything I want.

But most importantly, you gave everyone on your land one wish. I was currently on your land and was granted one wish. I didn't need it, so I wished you had powers when you just said you wished you had powers. Have a nice night, Danny."

Danny drove off with his mouth slightly agape. The look of shock Danny had was funny to Finn. However, he didn't entertain that image for long because he ran inside to tell his wife about Danny's wish for them both.

Rosea was waiting for Finn as he rushed into the house.

"Guess what, Dear? I ..." Finn stopped talking as he saw that Rosea had two bags packed.

Finn asked, "What's going on?"

"Well, when you are ready. We will leave here and go back in time and raise our Daughter. I understand how we can get Aislinn to become human and raise her. So go pack your bags." Rosea said as she looked at Finn.

Finn felt the urgency of his wife's direction. So Finn snapped his fingers and had two packed bags ready to go. Both bags bulged and had a metallic sound of gold coins shifting inside.

At that moment, Lyreman opened the door without knocking.

"You won't stop me, Lyreman. I know I can do this. I know things I didn't know earlier. The way to save Aislinn came to me an hour or so ago. I know what to do." Rosea said, seeming to want to rush away.

"Hold on just a few moments. I just need to talk to you two for a few minutes. Before you rush off, I need to tell you what happened. Danny's wish has granted the two of you power, but you need to know this. It will help you; I am sure you are blind to this information. So please listen.

If the both of you go now. You might not have Aislinn again in the future. She will be born, but maybe not by you. It is tough to say. Both of you feel powerful. I felt the pulse when that wish made you equal to me. The two of you were this powerful in the past, and it destroyed you. It had something to do with Aislinn back then, also. Please do not leave. I beg you." Lyreman said as the two held hands and vanished.

Finn and Rosea both had any power they wanted. So they went into the past to find Aislinn. They didn't need to hold hands to time travel since Finn now had that power and any other he wanted.

Lyreman left Finn and Rosea's cottage and got into the Rolls. The Butler turned and asked, "Did they go?"

"Yes, they did.", Lyreman said with a heavy heart. "They wouldn't listen. All that new power, and they jump without thinking about the enchanted rules. The rules must be followed, or balance won't happen."

The Butler slowly drove off, "What will happen, Lyreman?"

"I already know that they will die in the past. They actually have already passed away. They lost all power, breaking enchanted laws, and became human when they tried pulling Aislinn out of the fairy dream world. That can not ever happen. Leaving the fairy dream world is the choice of the Fairy, and not even her parents can change that.

You were not serving me yet when they came back after Aislinn. They died of old age. I was hoping I could talk them out of doing this, but I knew they had already done it. I watched them grow old and die many times over the ages. They will lose all memory and start again. They have already been reborn, and we have encountered both so far. What they did was so bad that they almost did what I had to endure many centuries ago. They never learn. They are great people and do great things, but when they lose Aislinn. They sometimes make rash decisions that cause them to vanish. No matter what I do, they keep bumping into themselves at different times. I can not stop them from repeating this same mistake. It's a good thing Finn took his gold coins with them. They needed it to live with." Lyreman replied.

"We have met them before? Who were they? I don't remember them." The Butler said as he sped down the road.

"I know it might seem odd, but Little Anders is Finn, and Rosea is actually the Fairy spirit that visits my cottage and thinks I am her brother. You know her as Joyce. The two will likely find each other again and have Aislinn as always. I hope they didn't mess it up so much this time that they don't have Aislinn because I adore her. She has been my friend through the centuries. She is like the Granddaughter I never had. At least, it's the one I remember. I have no idea, even if I ever had a child. I remember many things, but maybe I wasn't allowed to remember if I once had a child. And unless I ever meet someone whose spirit is meant to be with me again. I will stay single. Especially since a human killed the love of my life, and she has never reappeared. That happened many years ago and is hard to remember, which isn't normal for me.

Due to my status, I must help everyone, and the responsibility requires me to keep our world balanced. And Aislinn might even be my Grandaughter, but I have no idea, and my Father won't tell me her importance. Well. I hope they didn't mess up Aislinn coming back. I miss her already. I hope to stop Oisín and Niamh from messing up the next time Aislinn is born. My main hope is to end this horrible mess they keep repeating." Lyreman said as The Butler approached his cottage and drove over the small cobblestone bridge going to it.

"Oisín and Niamh? Oh, yeah. I forgot those two are Finn and Rosea. Too bad they don't keep the same names each life as Aislinn." The Butler said as he stopped and Lyreman got out.

"I agree. It does get confusing at times." Lyreman said this as he closed the car door, and then The Butler drove off.

Lyreman retreated to his cottage, making plans to help Little Anders. Since the boy's parents were dead, and Aislinn was one of them. He knew he needed to ensure Anders grew up with good values, and this time, he could influence him not to make such rash decisions. He was already helping a Fairy who lived most of the time in the fairy dream state. And Lyreman knew she would be Aislinn's Mom. Because she was Rosea and Little Anders was Finn, Lyreman couldn't predict the future, but he knew spirits and who they were.

Back on Danny's farm, Danny was surprised that his wife was fine with the Leprechaun and Fairy talk. His children were excited. And when Danny questioned if they would tell anyone at school about it. They surprised him by saying they would never tell others about it because the Little People were their family, and they must protect them. At that point, he realized his wish had come true.

Danny realized he finally knew things he didn't before and asked his wife, Heather, whatever had happened to her real parents.

She said, "I actually knew my parents. They had me, and I never disappeared when I was the age of five. They dropped me off with the lady who raised me down the road. They never came back for me. From what I remember from my childhood, they went to find my older sister. Then, when Finn and Rosea ate dinner with us one night, I realized they were my parents, but they didn't remember me. It didn't affect me since I knew they might not have had me yet. I am glad I got to see them, but I will never see them again. Yet, somehow, I am okay with that. It seems it should be this way. I hope they find my sister since they always were trying to do something to get her back, and nothing seemed to work. My human Mom never asked if they would take me back when Finn visited the farm asking questions. I think she knew he didn't recognize me. My real Mom always seemed unique. I believe she is enchanted, but she never indicated that she was. And my real Mom is the lady who raised me. I hold no negativity against Finn and Rosea because they were panicked, thought they could save one of their children, and put me somewhere safe while they did. I may never see them again. And that saddens me, but from what I understand. Enchanted people always see each other again eventually. At least in another life."

Finn and Rosea's cottage fell into disrepair as the years passed. Although, the fairy orchid grove thrived better than it ever had. Lyreman visited Danny and Heather often. He eventually told Heather that her parents could never return to her time. He told her he believed she would see them again, but they would not know her. She was very accepting like many enchanted were. This saddened Lyreman since he tried to tell them Heather was their child and her children were their grandchildren. But the enchanted world always tried to balance things. There was only so much magic and only so many magical spirits. So, for most, forgetting was part of how things balanced. Without that, many would suffer what Lyreman had to endure. And he wished he didn't have to, but being a child of one of the original enchanted came with abilities, even if they were hard on the owner. And for the most part, Lyreman always remembered most things, but the last hundred or so years seemed fuzzy. He could never figure out why that was.

When Little Anders was old enough to reopen his parent's restaurant, he was given access to a bank account saved from when he was younger that was in his parents' name. He didn't know that Rosea had deposited all that money that Dawn had stashed in their cottage into that account and put it under his parents' names with him as the primary recipient. She wanted her grandson to have a good life. Even though it was to help out Aislinn's son, she had no idea that Little Anders was Finn, who had returned because he passed away when they got stranded in the past. As odd as it was, Finn returned and was known as Little Anders. Lyreman decided never to tell Anders about his history. That was the mistake he made in the past. He would never tell Oisín and Niamh who they were when they came back ever again. He decided if Aislinn had any chance of a long and natural life again. They couldn't know. And any story of their past might give them ideas, and Lyreman could have them mucking up everything again. Little Anders was Finn, Aislinn's son, and this was extremely weird even for Lyreman, who had seen many odd things. Finn was Aislinn's Dad, but she would now be his mother. Finn and Rosea had really made a mess out of time and where spirits ended up. It was enchanted spirits, and they had to return in a body, but even Lyreman was concerned. He was worried that this time, the tampering that happened would stop Aislinn from ever existing again.

One time, while young Little Anders' Uncle took him to the grove when, many tiny fairy slipper orchids bloomed. Little Anders started to pick the orchid flowers. Something his Uncle was lightly upset about. But after Anders stated he wished to put them on his parent's grave. The Uncle did not object and picked a few himself.

At the grave, Anders sprinkled the orchids on the grave site. Which was mainly to his Mom, but his Dad was also part of it. His mother just overshadowed his Dad, and his Dad planned this since he gloried being married to the most beautiful and caring woman anyone had ever known.

And even as a little boy, Anders wished he could one day be married and love someone as his parents loved each other. And he hoped if he ever had children, that one would be like his Mom. He missed her ever so much.

Before driving from the grave site, Anders's Uncle handed him an odd gold coin, telling him he could never spend it and that it would be handed on when he finally had a son. Anders stared at the strange coin and, at one point, looked up to see the car approaching the old flower lady by the roadside in town. He thought that she needed the money much more than he did. Anders asked his Uncle to stop. He got out and asked the lady for the biggest bunch of yellow daisies she had. Then, the little boy tried to hand her the gold coin. The lady insisted that he keep the coin and let her eat in his restaurant as payment when he was older. So Anders returned his coin to his pocket, where he would carry it for years. Those flowers magically stayed fresh until his next visit to his mother's grave.

When Anders was old enough, he reopened the restaurant. In remembrance of his parents, he held breakfast and dinners for anyone who needed food. Old Lady Brona - The Flower Lady, was always allowed to eat for free, along with anyone in need.

"Lyreman, are you ever going to tell him?" The Butler asked as they watched Brona heading to get her free dinner one night at the Faerie Aislinn.

"I can't. Anders can never know I pretend to be his Uncle. I even change my looks to ensure he has someone to care for him, and I also drive a car to play that part. I have done this for countless people, and since Finn is now Little Anders, I will care for him, too. That is, until I fake my death again when I am no longer needed. That will be tough on him, but it needs to be done, and it is getting time for me to disappear."

"That seems so cruel. You are all that little boy has, Lyreman. You were the one who told him his parents had died. And you will take away his Uncle also?" The Butler said.

"I hear your concern, but Anders caries that gold coin daily. So he is drawn to our way of life, and I will replace the losses in his life one day." Lyreman stated.

The Butler stopped the vehicle, turned around, and looked at Lyreman, "How can you replace a person you pretend to kill off? Your intentions are always good, but it seems cruel this time."

Lyreman laughed and said, "Oh! I won't just fill in the void left by the loss of his Uncle. You will be part of it also. However, I am fuzzy for some reason as to why. But I am optimistic about the results."

"How can you be so positive if you are fuzzy on things? You are never fuzzy!" The Butler asked.

Lyreman sat back, lit his pipe, and took a puff,

"I am not sure, but I am positive that you do somehow.

Call it an intuition."

deireadh

Made in the USA
Columbia, SC
04 December 2023

dae5236a-8016-4f4c-9a3d-d11c2d583d95R01